Calder School

Under the WIDE BLUE SKY

Alberta Stories to Read and Tell

edited by LISA HURST-ARCHER
for THE ALBERTA LEAGUE ENCOURAGING STORYTELLING

illustrations by HEATHER URNESS

Red Deer PRESS

Published by
Red Deer Press
Trailer C
2500 University Drive N.W.
Calgary Alberta Canada T2N 1N4
www.reddeerpress.com

Credits
Edited for the Press by Lisa Hurst-Archer and Peter Carver
Copyedited by Lee Shenkman
Cover and text design by Erin Woodward
Cover image courtesy iStock
Printed and bound in Canada by Friesens for Red Deer Press

Acknowledgments
Financial support provided by the Canada Council, the Government of Canada through the Book
Publishing Industry Development Program (BPIDP), the Alberta Foundation for the Arts, a beneficiary of
the Lottery Fund of the Government of Alberta, and the University of Calgary.

   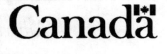

THE CANADA COUNCIL | LE CONSEIL DES ARTS
FOR THE ARTS | DU CANADA
SINCE 1957 | DEPUIS 1957

National Library of Canada Cataloguing in Publication
Under the wide blue sky : Alberta stories to read and tell / edited
by Lisa Hurst-Archer ; for the Alberta League Encouraging Storytelling ;
illustrations by Heather Urness.
Short stories.
ISBN 0-88995-324-4
1. Tales--Alberta. I. Hurst-Archer, Lisa II. Urness, Heather III.
Alberta League Encouraging Storytelling IV. Title.
PS8329.5.A4U64 2005   398.2'097123   C2005-901730-9

For our mothers and fathers and those who,
whether known or unknown to the world,
have told their story—may we have ears to listen.

ACKNOWLEDGEMENTS

Thanks to those whose stories have enriched my life, and who gave various kindnesses to this project at different points along the way: Mary Hays, Christina Pickles, Anne Cowling, Marjorie Russell, Pearl-Ann Gooding, Catherine MacKenzie, Cathie Kernaghan, Jean Burgess, Roberta Kennedy, and Keith Archer. Karen Gummo was an original and continual enthusiast and supporter of this project. I am grateful to Peter Carver of Red Deer Press for gentle encouragement and helpful support.

This book would not be possible without a supporting grant from The Alberta Lottery Fund Community Initiatives Program and continued support from The Alberta League Encouraging Storytelling.

CONTENTS

INTRODUCTION

Lisa Hurst-Archer

Every human being is a living treasure house of stories. The thousand and one tales tucked away in each of our hearts are our most precious possessions, and to give voice to them is a powerful assertion of our identity and our presence in the world.

We are, every one of us, storytellers. We tell about our childhoods, about finding new homes. We speak of our adventures, our deepest friendships, our meetings with strangers, our work, our leisure. We yarn about aunts and uncles, about exploits that make each family its own empire. We muse about our good fortune, our sorrows, our loves, our losses. The stuff of our lives is woven through the stories we tell and re-tell, develop and embellish.

Our storytelling speaks of who we are as individuals, as families, as members of communities. We pass along the stories of who we are and how we live and make sense of the world to future generations. All cultures possess a rich mixture of living wisdom, history, and humour in stories that are told round the hearth, on the street, in private and public places.

The Alberta League Encouraging Storytelling exists to celebrate and preserve the richness that can be found in our storytelling heritage. This collection of tales springs from the oral tradition of storytelling. Many of the stories have not previously appeared in written form; rather they have been developed orally. Most of the stories are *true* in that they arise from personal experience. A few are stories that have been held and protected and passed on from generation to generation. All have been told aloud to someone.

The told story is not the same as a written story. For one thing, the voice of the teller is what informs the story; in each of these stories you hear a distinct and compelling voice. If you were to listen at the kitchen table or at a storytelling concert, you would be struck by the tone, rhythm, gesture, and glance of the storyteller. The living dynamic of the oral tradition is the human voice. Our aim in this collection is to make sure that the oral medium—the living voice, as well as the stories themselves—is acknowledged and safeguarded; in that way, future generations will have access to the voices of those who might not otherwise be heard.

9

The stories represent a wide variety of voices. Some are from novice tellers; others from seasoned professionals. We have cast our net wide to include storytellers from all across Alberta, from rural and urban areas, stretching from Standoff in the south to High Level in the north. Some of the stories come to Alberta like seeds in a pocket, from other parts of Canada or from across the Atlantic. First Nations' people, settlers, and present-day immigrants are bound to one another through the common legacy of oral storytelling. All came here at one time from somewhere else, some recently, some long ago. Whether one came empty-handed, or with a small bundle, or a wooden cart, or a container loaded with goods, all came with a story. These stories help complete our understanding of place; Alberta, like Canada, is a place where people still come to make a new home, bringing stories with them. If we gather stories twenty-five years from now, we will hear different voices, from different places; we will have changed.

It is fitting to publish this collection in the year of Alberta's 100th birthday. We celebrate our common heritage of storytelling and encourage readers to participate in its flourishing.

Open the book in your hand to any one of these stories. Read it—then speak it aloud. Hear the storyteller's voice. And then, sometime later, sitting by the fire, around the kitchen table, or in a café, open the stories of your own life. Give voice to your own story. Become the storyteller.

GOOD GIFTS

THE GIFT OF STORY

Betty Hersberger

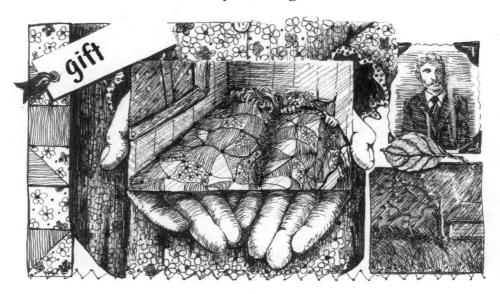

We are a family of nine, with nineteen years separating the eldest and youngest child. And we are a family of storytellers. Whether or not we were present at an event or even yet born, stories become the gift we give each other, by which we know our family and ourselves.

My older sisters and brother tell of a Christmas in Maryland when Granddad got out his shotgun and threatened to scare off Santa by filling his pants with a load of buckshot. "Won't allow that old guy in the house. Gonna sit up for him." Shocked by this threat, three little Canadian grandchildren ran to tell their grand-mother who solved the problem by helping them tie Granddad to the bed.

The children, who slept on pallets in the hallway, were awakened Christmas morning by their grandfather's leaping across them with cries of: "I got 'im. I got that old guy!" Of course he hadn't. Of course Santa had come and gone, leaving presents and candy, just as he had the Christmas before.

That's the shape of the story as I hold it. If you were to ask any of my sib-lings, they would probably shape the story differently. Although I have seen pho-tographs of my grandfather, I have no memory of him. But I have the story. I can hear his southern accent as he makes the threats. I can see him pretend to struggle against being tied up by three small children and their grandmother. I can see his lean body leap across my three sleeping siblings. Because I have the story, I have my grandfather.

Another story tells of how Dad taught each of his children to love a prairie storm. Sitting on the veranda with a child in his lap, he would count aloud the seconds between the lightning flashes and the thunderclaps. The relentless prairie wind would roll dark clouds across the sky, bringing the smell of rain and expectation. The number of seconds counted between the lightning and thunder would become fewer and fewer. Then the lightning flash would be directly overhead, giving unfamiliar shadows to familiar objects. The simultaneous thunderclap seemed to reach inside us. But we were safe with Dad under the shelter of the veranda and the protection of the lightning rod atop our roof.

I'm not sure that I ever was the child in that story. I might have been. I had watched storms from our veranda. I knew the safety of Dad's lap. I knew about counting between the lightning and thunder. But did I learn that from Dad or from the story?

In many of our stories, members of another family, the Rennicks, appear. June Rennick was in my grade at school. Colleen Rennick was in the same grade as my older brother Russ. Margaret Rennick and my youngest sister Kathy were born within five months of each other. At one family gathering, Kathy told the story of a time when Margaret Rennick had come for a sleepover.

"We're in the north bedroom," she began, "and, as usual, we're yacking and giggling enough for Mom or Dad to yell up to us to 'settle down up there!' Of course we don't—we just try to be a little quieter about how much noise we're making. There's a huge rainstorm that night and a really strong wind, so the rain is really pelting the windows. The rain sounds more like hail. It's kind of exciting at first, but you know what those storms are like. The wind makes the windows rattle and whistle, and of course it's pitch black because it's before we got the yard light. We're scared silly already, and then it does begin to hail."

The story of this hailstorm had been told many times before, but I had never heard Kathy tell it. I sat back to listen.

"The hail is just pelting the windows, like someone firing rocks or something at us, and we're fast figuring out that the windows just might break. I shout to Margaret over the thunder of the hail, 'It's gonna crash through the window!'

"Margaret screams back at me, 'Get under the covers!'

"We dive under the covers and curl up our legs as close to our bodies as we can. The window breaks and we feel the glass and the hail hit the bed. We're terrified.

"'Get the hell out of here!' We pop out our heads and see Russ in his underwear standing in the doorway shouting. Now I know this is serious because nobody in our house ever swears and nobody ever walks around in their underwear. Serious or not, I'm not going to cut my feet, so I make sure I don't walk in front of the window to get to the door, but Margaret takes off. We race downstairs to Mom and Dad's room. Mom checks our feet and I'm annoyed that in spite of my care, my feet are cut (not badly) and Margaret's aren't. And it isn't just our room that's hit; turns out that there isn't a bit of glass left in any of the windows on the north side of the house."

I waited until Kathy had ended her story. She had told the story almost exactly as I would have told it, with a difference in only a few details.

"Good story, Kathy," I smiled, "but it wasn't the north side of the house, it was the west side; it wasn't Margaret Rennick, it was June Rennick, and it wasn't you, it was me."

She looked at me, puzzled. She hesitated, and said, "I'm sure it was Margaret and me. I must have been there that night because I remember it."

And so she does. And so do I. We both have become the child in the story, hiding with a friend under the covers. One of us has given the story to the other. Knowing which of us gave the gift does not matter. It matters only that both of us hold it.

THE BEAR WHO STOLE THE CHINOOK*

Louis Soop

I had the pleasure of talking with Louis and Abby Soop about the value of growing up surrounded by stories. Abby's eyes shone as she remembered how her family gathered around the potbellied stove on cold, overcast Newfoundland evenings. The youngest children sat on the floor, the older children behind them, their parents listening in the background. They adjusted the stove so the glow of the firelight cast its spell over the family. Abby still can see the fire reflected in her father's eyeglasses as her sisters enthralled the family with tales of kings and queens and magical creatures.

Louis Soop grew up on the prairie at Standoff near the Belly River in Napi's garden, where the Blood Reserve is bordered by the Porcupine Hills and the Rocky Mountains to the west. His home was a two-room shack with few comforts: a straw mattress to sleep on, a wood stove, a few chairs, and a well-worn path out back.

*A retelling of a traditional Blackfoot tale.

Louis thought back to when the elders came to visit his mother. They sat on the living room floor and exchanged stories. Louis and his brothers were always at their mother's side even though they were encouraged to go outside to play. They found the warmth of the stories more comforting than the broad expanse of the great prairie. The brothers looked in on the visitors through the thick clouds of cigarette smoke and listened as the music of the Blackfoot talk was accented by periodic hand claps, the fluid sign language of gestures and the tap-tap of the tea cups signaling for more tea please, with one – two – three – four – five spoons of sugar.

"Matstsikii siksikimii – ni'tokskaa - naato'kaa – niookskaa – niisoo - niisita napiinawani."

Louis remembered how the elders adjusted the stories to the audience, time, and space—presenting a spare story or a generous tale. He learned how his world could be brought together in stories through explanations of the natural world, a comic view of human nature, bawdy humour, and respect for all living things. Here is a story told by Louis.

This is a story of a long time ago, in the Blackfoot country, way back . . . .

It was a time when there was nothing but cold weather. It was freezing in the morning and even got colder at night. People were shivering, cold, and miserable. The storms were not like now. The storms were *omahkokoyisttsomokana—big, furry, wolf-skin hat storms.* Now that is a powerful storm!

In the village there was one little teepee where a small boy lived all by himself. He was a friend to the birds and the animals. The boy thought he could do something about the situation. It was getting so bad that the dogs were skinny and the horses were starving. So he said to himself, "I will find out what is going on.

I will meditate." He burned sweetgrass and prayed. His friend Coyote came to pray with him. They were both meditating when along came Otter and Magpie. They all sat there wondering how they could bring an end to the big storm, *omahkokoyisttsomokana.*

The boy said, "First I will share the little food I have with you." After they ate the food and discussed the problem, the boy said, "I will perform a miracle." He took his drum and started to sing, "Hiyyaa, hiiyaaa, heyyaa, howyaa, heey heeeya, heeya."

Magpie is nosy and inquisitive. He always knows what is going on. Magpie said, "I think I know what is wrong. I happened to fly by a cave and there was a monstrous bear hibernating in the cave. He might have something to do with the storm. Bear has a great big buckskin bag. Whatever is in the bag is causing the terrible storm and the cold. We have to find Bear and his buckskin bag."

The boy and his friends traveled to the mountains to find Bear's cave. It was an exhausting journey. They slid down the valleys and clawed up the mountains. Their tongues were hanging out when they finally reached the cave. As they peered in, the boy instructed, "Coyote, you sneak in and find the bag."

So Coyote snuck into the darkness to steal the bag. He was just about to grab the bag, when Bear growled at him. Coyote took off! He was so scared. He exclaimed, "I cannot go in there again. Bear might eat me up."

Otter said, "I will go." He crept into the cave. When Bear growled at him, he took off. He was scared of Bear!

The boy asked Magpie to go and get the bag. Magpie replied, "The bag is big and I will not be able to pick it up."

The boy ordered, "You must try."

Magpie flew into the bear's den, as quiet as he could. He stole the big bag. To his surprise it was so light, like there was nothing in it. He took the bag to his friends and said, "We will take it home and show it to the medicine man. He will tell us what is in the bag, causing this bad winter."

When they got back home they went directly to the medicine man. He examined the bag and said, "There is something very, very suspicious in this bag. Everyone be careful and be prepared to run, when I open the bag." He slowly untied the buckskin bag. He opened the top, peered in — and what should come out?

"Shhhhhh . . . chinook!"

The material for the introduction was compiled by Mary Hays on a visit with Louis and Abby Soop in Pincher Creek, Alberta, on October 15, 2003. The story, "The Bear Who Stole the Chinook," was told by Louis Soop at a live concert on November 22, 2003, in Calgary. It was recorded with Louis' permission, transcribed by Mary Hays, and edited by Louis.

MRS. CAVE-BROWN

Jean Burgess

Mrs. Cave-Brown—the sound of her name gave my imagination limitless boundaries. I was drawn to unusual people when I was a child. Mrs. Cave-Brown was *very* unusual, and she lived with a charming, dapper, twinkly-eyed fellow named Dick Richardson, whom no one was certain was her husband. Or brother. Or cousin. In fact, neighbours gossiped that he was none of these.

   The pair lived in a log cabin high above the banks of a magnificent old river. Their home was larger than any I'd ever seen. The spacious surroundings of Mrs. Cave-Brown and Dick greatly added to the overall appeal of this couple. I never tired of going there with Father. Never had enough time to explore the long, rectangular living-dining room. Stuffed heads of antlered elk and mule deer reigned over the great room from their places on the walls, giving way here and there to an assortment of guns. Skins of cougars and wolves nested in front of easy chairs as if waiting for cold, tired feet. Bearskin rugs were scattered about the floor, so huge that if I stretched my child-body to its limit, fingers and toes never reached the edges.

   Above the fireplace mantel were sepia-toned photos of people. Who might these people be? Mrs. Cave-Brown's ancestors peering into her life? Some stared down ever so sternly and others seemed to say, "Look what she's up to now." The women in the photos were tall like Mrs. Cave-Brown and wore their hair in braids. For the men, it was obvious that a good measure of time was given to honing handlebar moustaches. I never saw a child in any of the photos on Mrs. Cave-Brown's walls.

Mrs. Cave-Brown's way of dressing was huggable. She wore vests and long skirts of tanned moose hide and always a red and blue tartan shirt. Beaded moccasins with tassels kept her tiny feet cozy. How could those feet—not much bigger than my four-year-old ones—hold up that towering woman?

Something that set her apart more than anything else, especially at that time in history, was that Mrs. Cave-Brown smoked. Women did not do that in the 1920s. Furthermore, she smoked a pipe! Father's face registered its high-cloud-cover-look when the topic of Mrs. Cave-Brown's smoking came up, though he held very strict views regarding the place of women in society.

I think the main reason we stopped by the Cave-Brown cabin by the river was that Father considered the woman's roasted moose meat irresistible. After a delicious meal he was satisfied and ready to leave—long before my eyes had feasted enough and before my imagination had gathered a full watershed of impressions to last until the next visit; before I was able to coax a smile from those faces gazing back at me from above the fireplace; before I'd had a chance to peek into all of the rooms.

"Jean never stops talking," I'd hear him say when we arrived home. "She tells the neighbours all my secrets."

I remember how Dick Richardson always adhered to Cave-Brown's wishes as if he were tethered by a strand of her long black hair. Our lady loved to have sheep around the way she had as a child in Scotland. Dick managed to procure a flock of sheep for her despite the dampness of the pastureland which resulted in the animals suffering hoof rot. It wasn't as serious as it might have been though; Cave-Brown had practiced as a veterinarian at one time. She deftly tossed a sheep on to its back, and held the animal while, following her instructions, Dick tended the hoof.

Father loved to visit the Cave-Brown household at butchering time. He'd had a chance to learn the butchering trade while serving in World War I and passed his skills on to Dick. However, I think he spent much of the time chuckling to himself while the bossy lady directed the operation. Dick jumped to her every order. In the end the work was done and we took home a huge roast of mutton to be popped into the oven, much to the delight of Father. He, too, had grown up in the Old World with sheep dotting far hillsides. Tantalizing lamb or mutton dishes were his mouth-watering favourites.

How Cave-Brown—sucking away on her pipe all the while—found time to make steamed, sponge puddings and scores of wild berry pies with their irresistible fragrance, I never figured out. I simply ate and enjoyed. I remember one aroma that permeated all the others. When she bent near me to serve up a slice of warm pie I could smell the smoky scent of the tanned moose hide clothing that she was wearing.

As soon as the river froze solid, neighbourhood men knew it was hunting time. Across the river from Cave-Brown's log cabin was untamed wilderness with deer, moose, cougar, and bear. At this time of year Cave-Brown's spreading farmstead became a stopping-by place as hunters journeyed to and fro. However, she never invited anyone to sleep inside her home. A large shed with the pelts of wild animals spread on the floor served as a bunkhouse for the hunters. Thus, no one ever did get answers to the questions: *Are they married? Do they share a room? Do they tumble in and out of the same bed?*

One year, Father persuaded Mother to let him join a hunting trip. He would stop at Cave-Brown's on the journey there and back. If lucky he would bring home a deer, perhaps a moose even. We all knew that canned wild game was tender and could be made into delicious stews or meat pies with deep rich brown gravy.

I picked up on Father's excitement as he loaded his sleigh with woollen blankets, food that Mother had prepared, and some of his finest oat bundles for his favourite team. I shadowed his every movement; my entire being suggesting silently: *Jean could sleep at Mrs. Cave-Brown's while you're out hunting across the river.* Silently I held my wish to my heart and he did not pick up on it.

It was Father's first and last hunting trip. Forever I will see his blood-stained blankets crumpled in the back of the sleigh on his return. His face was lined and grey and looked much older than it had on his departure. I stayed awake purposely that night. When I was in bed I heard him tell Mother what happened.

Three of his companions (without his knowledge) had taken along some homebrew. On a brilliant moonlit night the men slipped out of camp for a midnight hunt. One was shot accidentally in the shoulder. It was Father's younger brother. The other two, in their drunken state, were too long getting the injured man back to camp. Hours passed before they reached Mrs. Cave-Brown's door. Once they got there, she removed the bullet. Then, with a fresh team of horses, she set out for the village doctor, fifteen miles away. She seemed always to know what to do.

Years later I visited Mrs. Cave-Brown just before I set out for college. She was not striding from one end of the kitchen to the other, puffing away on her ever present pipe, the fragrance of fresh-baked berry pie in the air. Nor was she out tending sheep with foot rot or saddling up the team. Instead, she rocked on the veranda of her cabin gazing far off across the magnificent Wapiti River. Her braid was loosened. Nearly white hair cascaded across her shoulder and flowed downwards. The pipe lay on the table at the end of her outstretched arm, not even lit.

Through the years and the busy times of raising a family I thought often of Mrs. Cave-Brown and of the wealth of her being that she shared so freely to gift my childhood years. I wish now that I had kept in touch with her.

I am trying to pick up Mrs. Cave-Brown's trail. I am searching to follow her river of life to its end. How did she live out her last years? I question older people who knew her. I have many questions. Seventy years later I am still that child who longed for more time in her presence.

WHERE IS THE GOLD?

Karen Gummo

In marble halls as white as milk
Lined with a skin as soft as silk
Within a fountain crystal clear
A golden apple doth appear
No doors are there to this stronghold
Yet thieves break in to steal the gold.*

What is it?
Where is the gold?

Here is a story given to me by my mother Helen and my Auntie Pearl. I give
great thanks to them for this not so black-and-white tale. It is a story about
thieves and gold and eggs. However, the eggs were not the eggs with marble

---

*Traditional Riddle

halls as white as milk. These eggs were greyish- green, heavily spotted with brown. These were magpie eggs.

Helen and Pearl Swainson found themselves in the middle of a family of ten children, growing up on a farm along the old Burnt Lake Trail west of Red Deer. They had enviable freedom as young children to roam the countryside as long as their chores were done. And so they did, wandering off to Mrs. John's to hear gossip around the swill pail, or into the bushes to build wild, willow-branch forts. When they were about ten and eleven years old in the early 1940s, common wisdom had it that the magpie and the crow were a menace to the planet, and especially to the farmers. They had to be eradicated. Local municipalities and sports clubs offered a reward of a penny per egg. Helen and Pearl saw this as a great opportunity. The sisters had few chances to line their pockets with gold (any coins would be like gold to these girls). Now opportunity came knocking.

Where is the gold? It's in the egg. Where is the egg? It's in the nest. Where is the nest? It's in the tree! Where is the tree? We shall see!

To set the record straight, Helen and Pearl weren't cruel-hearted young people. They had seen the fierce way that magpies robbed nests of the songbirds the sisters cherished. They had heard Kerry Wood, the local naturalist, tell of the magpie menace—those nasty creatures who willfully kill feeble newborn lambs, piglets, and calves by pecking their eyes out, then clamour around to feast on the remains. The girls had watched those daredevils steal feed from the animal troughs. Daily they observed those well-dressed birds parading about so haughtily, so noisily, planning their next attack. Who would not want to rid the world of so nasty a beast?

Helen and Pearl were not the first to enter this campaign against the magpie. Their older siblings and friends were veterans in this war. What territory could the girls explore that had not yet been robbed? The answer came to them simply, as a gift.

Not far from their home, and adjacent to the one-room schoolhouse they attended, lived a lonely Norwegian bachelor by the name of Mr. Gustafson, Gusty for short. This curious fellow lived in an unpainted one-room shack with no running water and no electricity. He definitely had a particular odour about him. Who knew when he had last taken a bath! They said his house was full of books;

that he slept on books, sat on books, ate off books, and read them a great deal too. It was concluded that he must be very clever. But what good was that? The books were all in Norwegian and he could hardly speak English. The sisters came from proud Icelandic stock, but they were Canadian now.

Every few months their parents would invite Gusty to dinner. Continuing the traditions of their Icelandic forebears, it was a practice in the community to care for anyone in need, and even odd old gentlemen like Gusty regularly received kind invitations.

One evening in June, when they were blessed with the company of their bachelor neighbour, Helen and Pearl had the job of clearing the table. A favourite game for them was to discreetly plug their noses in disdain as they passed behind the smelly fellow. Hiding in the kitchen they whispered, "Gusty, Gusty, you're so dusty, when will you take a bath!"

Then a thought occurred to one of the girls. Where could they find magpie nests undisturbed? They could find them at Gusty's place. Of course! His little shack was surrounded by a great copse of trees and bushes. Nobody went there. Gusty was a mystery man and a little unpredictable too. People made a point of not disturbing him. The wooded grove surrounding his shack might hold the treasure trove they were seeking!

The girls awoke at dawn the next morning. They had got word to their buddies, Lily and Marion, to come along for the adventure. They gathered in the silence of the morning. There were some equipment requirements for their work. They each donned a hat of some kind. They found some garden gloves and tucked those into a straw-lined Roger's Syrup pail where they would place the eggs for safekeeping. There would be no reward without evidence! They put a few hermit cookies into their pockets for a snack. Last of all, they gathered a most critical item, a good long ladder. This would be invaluable to them when the nests were found high up in a tree with few low branches.

Quietly they swung the ladder up on all their shoulders to share the load. Now they were literally linked in their mission. They began to make their way out of the family farmyard toward Gusty's place. They were not lucky enough to go undiscovered though. Older brothers, up early for chores, called out from the barn loft, "What's the ladder for, girls? Need some tree climbing lessons?"

The girls did not respond. They simply gathered their courage, puffed up their chests, and marched forth chanting: "Where is the gold? It's in the egg. Where is the egg? It's in the nest. Where is the nest? It's in the tree! Where is the tree? We shall see!"

In this manner, they made their way across the west pasture toward Gusty's place. When they reached the edge of his little wood, they set down the ladder and began to think things through. There were dangers to be considered. What if the mother magpies were at home? Wouldn't they be angry? Well, they could wave a stick and ward them off. If the eggs had hatched, what would they do with the babies? Some said Gusty kept a gun and would fire it off if unwanted strangers came too close. Would he fire the gun if he saw them? He never aimed at people; he only aimed up in the air to scare them off. It could be very scary, if he got sloppy with it, and . . . you know . . . .

Suddenly Helen noticed an enormous nest in a willow bush. It was huge, with a canopy covering the top. Those magpies are clever architects! No ladder needed here. The girls simply pulled on the branches and peered in. The nest was empty. Magpies often built their nests in colonies. They were hopeful they would not find a ghost town here. Hoisting the ladder back onto their shoulders, they ventured into the wood with their equipment at the ready.

There they saw a big tall poplar with a great bowl of twigs near the top. They stopped, gave the tree a little nudge and having received no answer, leaned the ladder against the sturdy trunk. Lily and Marion steadied the ladder while Pearl made the ascent. Helen was to keep watch for Gusty and respond to any dangers. Pearl placed her feet carefully on the lower rungs while grasping above until she was able to peer into the nest . . . empty.

Where is the gold? It's in the egg. Where is the egg? It's in the nest. Where is the nest? It's in the tree! Where is the tree? We shall see!

There was no sign of Gusty so they ventured further into the woods. Noticing a flutter of black and white overhead, they followed it to the tree where it landed. It was a great old tree with many high branches and a few down low, but it was quickest to make use of the ladder. Leaning it up against the trunk, they had a sense that this would be their lucky tree, especially when they heard the noisy chatter coming from on high. The girls craned their necks to see two long-tailed black and white birds alight on a nest of twigs.

"Mag! Mag! Mag!" the birds squawked and threatened.

Pearl grabbed a good strong stick and tied it onto her belt loop. She steadied herself and adjusted her hat. "Hold the ladder, girls—this could be a battle!"

Lily and Marion braced themselves, clutching either side of the ladder, and Pearl clambered up. Helen had been watching for Gusty but now her focus was on Pearl's skyward climb. Pearl reached the top of the ladder and then had to venture further upward, clinging to the trunk. Her footholds and handholds had to be precise now. Her muscles bulged from the effort. All that work with the men in the fields had prepared her well for this. Hoisting herself around the mass of sticks and twigs to a vantage point just above the nest, she found a treasure trove of magpie eggs!

"Helen, be quick, bring the bucket, we've hit the jackpot! I count one, two, three, four . . . seven eggs!" Pearl boasted.

Why didn't she bring the pail in the first place? Helen wondered as she followed her sister upward. She felt the tree sway as Pearl responded to the swoop of the mother magpie. Then the commotion began. There were several magpies zooming in to ward off the predators.

"Mag! Mag! Mag!" cried the angry birds.

One black and white menace knocked off Pearl's hat while another darted close. Pearl pulled out her stick and waved in self-defense. It was not easy to keep her composure in such a spot. How was she going to reach for the bucket, ward off her attackers, collect the eggs, and not fall out of the tree?

"Mag! Mag! Mag!" The cries came from all directions now.

"Out of the way, Helen! I'm coming down!"

The two of them made their way down in a frenzy, Pearl nearly landing on top of Helen. As they disentangled themselves and began to argue over bungled technique and strategy, Marion stopped them with a whisper.

"Look, it's Gusty, and he's got his gun!"

They noticed for the first time how close they had come to Gusty's little shack. Now he was standing barely fifty feet away. They dropped to the ground, bringing the ladder down on top of them.

The four girls pasted their sweaty bodies with wildly beating hearts as close to the ground as they could. Could he hear them breathing?

"Who goes there?" called the old man as he scanned the woods. Gusty waited and watched. The girls did the same. They could discern his shape through the underbrush.

Either his eyesight was not very good, or he chose not to see them. Setting his gun just inside the door of his house, he began to reach out to the mangle of magpies all around him. A chaotic fervour of cawing and squawking filled the air. Now Gusty was calming their frantic state. He began to hum and his song had a pacifying effect.

He sat in an elaborate, high-backed chair on the porch. The chair had knobby arm-rests curved like necks to round heads with beaks pointing left and right. The wooden legs were perched on clawed feet. Gusty's humming lulled the birds until their chatter ceased. The black-and-white birds gathered around him. One landed on his lap, hopped up to his shoulder and onto his hat. Gingerly, he leaned down to pick up a piece of wood and a knife. Humming some more, he began to whittle.

The girls were transfixed.

After some time he held up his carving to admire it. The girls could make out the shape of a . . . magpie!

He dropped his knife and now the bird that had been perched on his head came floating to the ground, picked up the knife in his talons, dropped it in Gusty's lap, and returned to settle atop the old man's hat. The old man worked intently for what seemed like ages.

At last he put down his carving and stood to stretch. Pulling some crumbs out of his pocket, he fed his feathered friends. He took one last scan of the woods and then disappeared into the shack that was his home.

Helen, Pearl, Lily, and Marion waited a few moments to see if Gusty would reappear outside. When he did not emerge they picked themselves up and stealthily made their way out of Gusty's wood.

When they were halfway across the west pasture toward home they began to have a lively discussion about what had just transpired.

"Gusty sure likes magpies!"

"That proves he's a crazy old man."

"They're beautiful and clever. When they turn a certain way there's blue and green in their black feathers."

"I still say they are nasty birds!"

"So are we—look what we tried to do today."

"Let's not talk about it. We won't tell anyone about this, will we?"

It was agreed. They all returned home. Their lips were sealed. They did not respond to queries from other family members about their adventures on that day.

Not more than two months later, who should be invited to dinner at the Swainson Farm but Gusty? Helen and Pearl were feeling uneasy about it. When at last they spied a small figure walking up the laneway, they peered out in amazement. He was dressed in a suit. Where did he get it? The jacket and pants were black and he wore a crisp, white shirt underneath. Somebody was taking care of him! He was carrying something too, some kind of homemade basket. Was he bringing gifts?

"Girls, I'd like you to greet him at the door when he arrives," called their mother.

"I don't feel well," said one.

"Neither do I," said the other.

"Helen and Pearl: please open the door!" called their mother who was busy stirring something on the stove.

They had to go to greet him, face to face.

Gusty smiled. "I brought you a gift."

The girls looked in the basket. It was full of eggs; they were greyish-green, heavily spotted with brown. The girls looked at one another.

"Take one," insisted Gusty.

Helen and Pearl each reached an uncertain hand into the basket and picked up an egg. They felt the smooth oval shape that fit perfectly into their palm.

Suddenly Helen dropped hers. It did not break! She bent down to pick it up.

Gusty laughed, "Do you like my carving?"

Of course, these were wooden eggs! Helen and Pearl smiled uneasily and slipped the eggs into a pocket.

In marble halls grey-green and brown
Lined with a skin like a silken gown
Within a fountain crystal clear
A golden apple doth appear
No doors are there to this stronghold
Yet thieves break in
And steal the gold

What *will* we be? Observer or intruder? Thief or friend?
Where *is* the gold?

THE PERFUME OF PEARS

Marie Anne McLean

I was watching a friend at work who had brought a pear in her lunch. As she sliced the pear and the juice ran down the knife, I thought of the way I used to love pears when I was little.

Pears are wonderful for a little kid. They are easy to bite into. They are juicy and messy and sweet. They have little bits of grit in them that seem to be sugar. They even have a perfume that smells as good as any cologne that Mom wears.

The other thing that made pears so special was their rarity. Nowadays you can find pears in the stores all year round. They are there in a variety of colours and kinds. But when I was little, they were only available during a brief window of about three or four weeks because of their fast-ripening fragility. They would come on the train in case lots. People bought them for canning, to put them away for the winter. Oh, you could buy them by the bag for eating, but we could never do that. That was an expensive way to buy them, and we didn't have money to spare.

It wasn't that pears were the only fruit we preserved. We had all the regular local fruits: strawberries, raspberries, saskatoons, and blueberries preserved in juice, jams and jellies and chokecherries and cranberries for syrup.

Then we would get exotics like peaches, apricots, and pears.

When the cases of pears came in, Grandpa would tell Grandma and Mom. He always knew when the first load arrived because his job was to meet the train and deliver all the freight in town.

We would get our case of fruit and we could have only a few pieces for eating fresh because of the expense. We needed to preserve them so that we wouldn't have to buy expensive factory canned fruit in winter.

The blitz of canning would begin. I had to help with it because there were many important jobs that my mom needed me to do. I lined up jars and washed fruit. When the peeling was done, the pits would go into the wood stove but the peels had to be taken out to the chickens. That was one of my important jobs. I loved the chance to go out into the shade beside the house and the chickens loved those fruit treats. They had a taste for those peach and apple peels. I don't know if they liked pear peelings because they never got any. I would take them out, sit in the shade, and eat them all myself.

I learned some interesting math facts when we canned fruit. Did you know that if you're careful, you can cut the pieces so that there are no leftover pieces of peach or apricot when you fill the jars, but it is not possible with pears?

Whenever we canned pears, there were always leftover pieces that my mom would get me to eat because we couldn't waste them. Each time I got a leftover piece, my mom would smile and say, "I don't know why that happens. I was never very good in math. I once got sixteen in Algebra." Then she would roll her eyes and laugh. It was funny because she could always add her whole grocery list in her head.

One summer the canning season seemed to just flatten my mom. It was always a hard time. The heat of a prairie summer was hard enough in our little two-room house without the addition of the heat of a wood stove boiling all those canning jars. But this time it was worse. My mom wasn't laughing or singing. She usually sang and made jokes and talked to me while she worked but that summer she was quiet and often went to the bedroom to cry. Dad was quiet too.

When I was older I learned the cause: there had been a baby coming but when it was about six or seven months along, instead of waiting to be born, it had died.

That summer's canning time was hot and joyless. On the Saturday that Grandpa told Dad that the pears were in, we were supposed to go to town in the wagon with Dad, who was hauling a last load of grain to sell. When it was time to go, Mom said she was too tired. This was a cause for concern. Saturday was when we went to the movies. Mom and I loved movies. If she was willing to miss a movie, she must be really sad. I would have to stay home to keep her company. I wasn't thrilled with that idea either.

After Dad left, Mom and I had a story and a snack and went to bed. She said I could lie down in the big bed until Dad came home. That, and the story, kind of made up for the missed trip to the movies.

We lay and talked until Dad came home. He came into the bedroom and said, "Why don't you come on out now that it is nice and cool?"

Mom sighed and said she didn't think she'd bother getting up.

"But I got you a nice cold bottle of Coke," Dad smiled.

Mom always loved Coca-Cola. It was her favourite, and a cold drink was always a treat because we had no refrigerator. So we both got up and went out to sit on the step. He had a cold bottle of Coke for each of us but none for himself.

Then he stepped over in front of the clothesline stand and said, "Guess what I got!" He had his jacket thrown over something on the stand. With a *ta-da* flourish like a ringmaster, he whipped the jacket away. Sitting on the clothesline stand was a cream-coloured, rectangular, metal box.

Dad said, "Watch this!" and opened the lid. Two sides folded out to hold the lid open. He took out a grill and a tank. The grill he replaced in the box. The tank he pumped with a little knob on a rod inside the end. After he judged he had pumped enough, he hooked the tank on the front of the box. Then he produced a match, which he struck on his pant leg, and lit the burner in the box.

"A camp stove," he smiled, "I thought you could use it for canning."

"How much did it cost?" Her voice was tired.

"Seventeen dollars."

"We can't afford seventeen dollars," she sighed.

"Oh yes, we can. I got a good deal on that load I sold." He was smiling even more.

That was when she looked up and said, "Brilliant!"

"I know!" He was laughing.

"That's so good, we should make toast." She stood up as she spoke and went back into the house.

Soon she returned with a cookie sheet for a tray, and on it the toast grill from the wood stove, bread, butter, jam, butter knives, and three glasses.

We split the cola three ways and then we made toast. As the sky darkened into night, we had a little celebration on the step.

And so I learned some lessons from my parents. Sometimes it is possible to get exactly the right gift for someone. And sometimes it is possible to receive exactly the right gift from someone. And when that happens you should acknowledge it with love and laughter and a celebration.

HARD TIMES

Calder School

DITCH OF DREAMS*

Helen Lavender

It was 1929 and life in Europe was hard. Good jobs were scarce. The fellows on Frank's roadwork crew were talking about going to Canada. Frank dreamed that he could go there, get a job, save money, and send for his wife and three sons later.

"There is a lot of work in Canada—land of opportunity," he overheard the others on his work crew scheming.

A few of the men resolved to go to Canada and begin a new life. Frank and his wife had long conversations in the evenings. Eventually they decided that Frank, too, would go. He sailed with the others across the wide Atlantic, then rode the rails west from Montreal. When the train stopped at Fort Saskatchewan, little money remained in his pocket, so he let the train go on without him.

He was glad to put his feet on the soil of this new land. Blue sky stretched high above him and touched the horizon wherever he looked. Frank was determined to make a go of it here and immediately he asked for work. He was

*This story was researched and developed for the 2000 Alberta Winter Games series of storytelling concerts as part of the TALES Strathcona Heritage Project.

directed to a local store and told to ask for Charles Thomas, who was looking for a farm hand.

"Mr. Thomas has not been in yet." The proprietor answered Frank's question. "He usually comes to town Saturday and he gets his groceries here. Set a bit and wait. Charles will show up by mid-afternoon."

Frank was nervous. He could not speak much English, though he understood most of what he heard. Some voices spoke German and some Polish, he thought as people came and went. When a large-framed man came lumbering through the door, the proprietor pointed to Frank.

"Charles, here's a man looking for work. Think he might be a ditch digger?"

Charles laughed. "That ditch is only a dream, George. A farm hand is what I need now. Have to get that crop in as soon as we can."

The large man strode across the wide, wooden floorboards and held out his hand.

"Hello, fellow. I'm Charles Thomas. I farm south of Josephburg. Looking for work, are you?"

Frank jumped to his feet, accepted the outstretched hand, and shook it firmly. The grip was friendly and made him feel welcome.

"Yes sir. I save money to bring family to live in good country."

"Where do you come from, Frank, and what work did you do?"

"I come from Yugoslavia. You know Yugoslavia? Not safe. No jobs. I good worker. Work on roads, canals. You need ditch? I dig ditch."

Charles laughed. Then his ruddy face turned serious.

"I don't need a ditch right now. I have a grain farm and cattle. I need to get the crop in and good help is scarce in these parts. What about your family, Frank?"

"I have wife and three boys. I save money and they come to Canada. Safe in Canada, yes?"

"Yes, Frank, I think it's safe in Canada. We have to work hard, but anyone willing to work can make a good life in Canada. Do you want to come out to the farm and have a look? We could see how you like the cattle and horses tomorrow."

Gladly Frank climbed into Mr. Thomas' farm wagon and accompanied him home where Charles' wife and two sons welcomed him.

"Three sons in my country," he told the youngsters. "Bring to Canada soon."

Frank was delighted to answer questions as best he could for the curious boys. He liked to tell them about his own sons and he demonstrated with his hand how tall each one stood. He missed his family in Yugoslavia.

Frank stayed on to work for Charles Thomas, and he put in long days until the crop was in. Charles was pleased with Frank's persevering manner and his able handling of stock and tools. It was several weeks before anyone mentioned a ditch, but Frank could hold his curiosity no longer. After supper one night he inquired about the "dream of a ditch" about which he had overheard talk on his arrival.

"Oh, that," chuckled Charles. "The neighbours have been kidding me about that for some time. The big slough in the west field covers a lot of my land. I once thought of ditching that water north along the side of the field, then east to the creek on the other side of the home quarter. It's the natural drainage route. But it's too big a job."

"Frank have a dream too," the new hired man suggested. "I dig ditch. My dream and your dream come true."

"How do you mean, Frank? I thought your dream was to save money to bring your family here."

"Mr. Thomas, I dig ditch for you every night after farm work done and I save money more quickly to bring family."

"Dig with what? I haven't any digging machinery or a team to spare. I can't afford to buy another team."

"I buy shovel, dig after work. After supper lots of time to dig. You pay what you want, half wages if you want. I not sit all evening and talk. You show me how big, where you want me to dig, I dig."

Mr. Thomas doubted Frank's plan. It was foolish to consider. It would take many days, many summers to dig such a ditch by hand. He didn't want to see his hired hand work that hard after a full day's honest work.

Frank was persistent and determined. He proposed low rates of pay. He talked and talked about his desire to work, his need to save every penny. He tried to convince Charles to draw up a contract. Charles refused but told him how much he would pay. The two men went to town to buy the shovelling and sharpening tools that Frank wanted. On a mild Sunday afternoon in May, Frank and Charles stood out in the field and surveyed the expanse of land. They marked out a line, using an ordinary carpenter's level, and determined the depth and width requirements along it.

The next evening after supper and chores Frank eagerly took his pick and shovel and walked alone across the field and began to dig.

We cannot know what Frank endured, what dreams and visions filled his mind and spurred his work. But we can go out on Charles' land and see that ditch. It runs nearly half a mile along the west side of that quarter section, a half mile across the bottom, through a culvert on a municipal road that has been built between the two quarters, and across the bottom of the next quarter. Here it turns along the east side of the second quarter, almost to the creek—a total of nearly two miles. It varies in depth from four feet to seven feet. It was dug by the hands of one man.

The ditch was finished and still Frank did not have enough money to send for his family. The turmoil in Europe in the late thirties worried Frank and the Thomas family. When Frank received news that two of his sons, now aged four-teen and sixteen years, were to be conscripted into the German army, Charles and others loaned him the money required for the family's passage.

Friends and relatives helped the family make their way to France, where at last they boarded a ship to sail for their new home. As is turned out, it was the last ship to leave Europe with emigrants before the start of World War II. As we know, Yugoslavia was aligned with Germany and a few days later Frank's sons would have been enlisted in the service of the Fuhrer.

The voyage was a horror for Frank's wife and second son as they were con-stantly seasick. They dragged themselves with great difficulty up to the deck to breathe in the fresh air. The constant rolling of the waves and the sight of water all around did not help. What a relief it was when they set foot on land once again.

We know it was a long journey west to Fort Saskatchewan, where they were met by Frank and the Thomas family. It had been ten long years of hope and sweat and determination. Frank had realized his dream.

The Thomas family still owns the land. They remember the man who left his mark—a long smooth hand-dug ditch. Tall poplars, grass, and brush grow in it today but it has not been filled in. It loudly proclaims the story of the hard work and determination of a man with a dream.

Frank and his family remained in the district, and eventually bought a farm near the Thomases where they raised their four boys. The youngest of

Frank's sons, John, and his wife Margaret were in attendance when I told this story at a concert in Josephburg in May of 2002. They were delighted to hear it. Frank's family and the Thomas family remain close friends. Warren Thomas still refers to Frank as Uncle Frank, and still speaks with admiration for the man who dug the ditch on the farm where he has raised his own family and still lives today.

THE QUEEN AND I

Mary Hays

The twenty-fourth of May
Is the Queen's birthday.
If we don't get a holiday
We'll all run away!

My personal connection with the Queen began as a child, chanting this rhyme, and with the story of how my mother had tea with Queen Elizabeth in England during World War II. My mom was raised on the bald prairie near Irricana, not far from Calgary. She and her two sisters helped their widowed mother make a go of it on the farm during the Depression. It was *the hard times* and they learned the lesson of *waste not, want not*. Mom and her twin sister worked hard on the farm to gather the resources to attend the University of Alberta. At the ripe age of sixteen years, they headed to Edmonton to study nursing. The twins graduated in 1938, dressed in matching white satin gowns.

The world changed in 1939 with the outbreak of World War II. Mom wanted to do her patriotic duty and join the Canadian Army. On her twenty-fifth birthday, she enlisted in the Royal Canadian Army Medical Corp as a nursing sister. To her great disappointment, she was posted to Currie Barracks in Calgary. She wanted to go overseas with her friends who were providing nursing care in casualty clearing stations and field hospitals on the battlefields of Europe. After a year of waiting, they got word that their hospital, No. 11 Canadian General, was to be mobilized for overseas duty. Preparations were made to organize the medical personnel for their new posting. Finally the day arrived. That day Mom was allowed to go home and have lunch with her mother. Due to military secrecy she was not allowed to tell her mother she was leaving for overseas duty. I can only imagine what that lunch would have been like, Mom not knowing if she would see her mother again: a sandwich, a bowl of soup, a cup of tea . . . a kiss goodbye.

The hospital personnel traveled in a troop train across Canada to Halifax where they boarded a luxury cruise ship, the *Queen Elizabeth*. Mom was billeted in a suite with twenty-five other nursing sisters who slept on bunks stacked three high. There were 13,000 medical personnel on their ship. They were part of a convoy that zigzagged across the stormy North Atlantic to evade the German submarines. Once they arrived safely, they traveled to Lord and Lady Astor's estate near Taplow in southern England. Mom became the assistant matron of No. 11 Canadian General Hospital.

During the spring of 1944, there was a great troop buildup in southern England. The troops were undergoing long marches to build their stamina and exercises to test their skills: map and compass reading, aircraft identification, cliff climbing, water manoeuvres, and waterproofing vehicles. Every afternoon, the Allied bombers flew directly over Mom's hospital, relentless in their assault on industrial Germany. Every morning, the bombers would return in imperfect formation with crippled stragglers dangerously sputtering behind. The steady drone of bombers was a constant reminder of war.

On D-Day, June 6, 1944, the long awaited invasion of Europe began. The Allied forces landed on the beaches of Normandy to push through France into Belgium, Holland, and Germany. With the battles came the casualties. The young soldiers—seventeen, eighteen, nineteen, twenty years old—fell to 88 mm shells and artillery fire. Initially, there was not room for field hospitals at the front, so the wounded were taken from the battlefields by stretcher-bearer to field ambulances and then evacuated by air transport ambulances to Canadian hospitals in southern England.

No. 11 Canadian General Hospital was ready for the onslaught of wounded. The medical staff at Mom's hospital worked non-stop. They admitted and cared for two hundred casualties a day. The boys arrived with terrible injuries: penetrated chests and abdomens, broken bones, concussions, and eye injuries. The young men—who had been fighting on the beaches and in the trenches of Normandy— also needed the basics: a meal, a clean bed, a bath, a shave, and a Red Cross kit bag of essentials.

The thirty-six hospital wards overflowed with five hundred patients. Two weeks after D-Day, amid the intensity of this work, they received news that Her Majesty Queen Elizabeth had chosen to visit No. 11 Canadian General Hospital! Preparations for the royal visit were made: the hospital was cleaned until it shone, the beds were made to military precision, and the patients were prepared.

At the appointed hour, a limousine pulled up to the hospital and out stepped the Queen, accompanied by her entourage, including the Rt. Hon. Vincent Massey, Canadian High Commissioner, Major-Generals Montague and Luton, and Lady Astor. The Queen travelled up and down the wards. She took time to speak to every soldier, thanking each one for his great sacrifice in the effort to bring peace to the world. Each young man felt a personal connection with the Queen as she gracefully moved through the hospital. She was a picture of elegance, dressed in a powder-blue two-piece suit, tastefully accessorized with a strand of pearls and a diamond maple leaf pin given to her by the Canadian people. She wore a stunning hat: blue felt featuring a dramatic, contrasting bow.

As the Queen visited one ward, she passed by a young soldier who was fumbling to balance his crutch and his camera in an attempt to snap a picture of Her Royal Highness. She could see his dilemma. She paused, posed, and inquired thoughtfully, "Did you get your photo?" The boy was swooning as he nodded, "Yes, Your Majesty."

It was a gruelling afternoon, having to speak attentively to all those injured young men. After several hours, General Luton grew weary and attempted to usher the Queen past a closed ward door. But Queen Elizabeth was very systematic. She noticed the door and asked, "Are there wounded boys behind that closed door?"

The general humbly replied, "Yes, Your Majesty."

She insisted, "We must not miss anyone, no matter how badly injured they are. Let us proceed!"

On they went, the Queen charming everyone with her captivating smile.

The nursing sisters were honoured when the Queen accepted their invitation to join them for afternoon tea in Lady Astor's hunting lodge. Each of the fifty nurses was presented to the Queen. She thanked them for doing their part in the reconstructive work of war. Her sweet smile and gentle manner made my mom, a farm girl from the prairie of Alberta, feel she had a personal connection with royalty.

They were told the war would be over by Christmas 1944, but the war raged until May 1945. At the end of the war, Mom was posted to a hospital in Holland. This was a different kind of nursing. They looked after the boys who were being demobilized back to Canada where they would take up civilian life. There was time for tennis games, parties, dances, sightseeing, and trips to the theatre. It was in Holland that my mom, Nettie, met Fred, a dashing young dentist who had served out the war with the Royal Canadian Army Dental Corps.

Well, you know how it goes. *First comes love . . .* Fred and Nettie returned to Calgary. *Then comes marriage . . .* They settled into civilian life in Olds, Alberta. *Then come Fred and Nettie with the baby carriage!* They had three lovely children. I am the baby of that family.

As we grew up, Mom told us the story of when she had tea with the Queen. She encouraged us to sit up straight at the dinner table and to use polite table manners just in case the Queen stopped by for a cup of tea. This was perfectly logical to us kids; our mother had had tea with the Queen in England and so if the Queen came to Canada she would most likely stop for tea at our house in Olds. We expected her visit. Just as our mother did, we felt a personal connection with the Queen.

It wasn't until my husband and I raised our own two children and I told them the story of how their grandmother had tea with the Queen that I discovered the truth of the story.

After all those years of waiting and waiting for the Queen to knock on our door and join us for tea, I realized that the Queen had been with us every day. She was robed in a sensible house dress and a cotton apron as she served us, with royal grace and charm, meat loaf and scalloped potatoes.

HOW BLACKIE AND I HELPED WIN THE WAR

Vic Daradick

In 1944, when I was a young boy only seven years old, I became very influenced by an old black horse. It was in the middle of those awful years of World War II. My father was away doing his patriotic duty as a naval officer on the *S.S. Buckingham* escorting merchant ships across the ocean to England and back again.

In the meantime, my mother dragged little sister and me from place to place as she worked as a domestic helper on farms or wherever she could work and keep her little children. One of the places mother worked was on Mr. Rash's ranch in southern Alberta. Mr. Rash had two sons who were in the air force fighting that awful war. So Mr. Rash was left at home with his wife to run the ranch. It wasn't long before I was recruited into becoming one of the ranch hands. Boy! I was so proud that the buttons nearly popped off my shirt. Mr. Rash saw right away that his horse, old Blackie, and I got along pretty good, so he asked me if I thought I could manage to keep the cows out of the oat field.

But now I'm getting ahead of my story. As soon as I got to the farm I fell in love with old Blackie and wanted to ride him. So one day Mr. Rash saddled him

43

up and showed me how to ride him. Mr. Rash was a busy man and didn't have time to saddle up old Blackie every day so the horse and I got well enough acquainted on our own, and I soon learned how to ride him bareback. But I had not yet learned how to put the bit in his mouth. Mr. Rash soon informed me that if I was going to ride old Blackie I would have to ride him in the proper manner. I would have to learn how to put the bit into Blackie's mouth. I very soon learned how to put the bit into his mouth and then I could steer old Blackie around wherever I wanted. When Mr. Rash saw this, he figured I might as well put all that energy to good use. So he soon directed me down to the far end of the pasture to bring back the cattle.

Now Mr. Rash had about sixty head of cattle, but two of them were brought in every night for milking and then let out in the morning to feed in the pasture with the other cows. For some reason, the cows always seemed to be at the far end of the pasture every afternoon when I went to get them. Of course, I couldn't cut out just the two milk cows so I had to drive the whole herd up to the barn where Mrs. Rash would call in her two pet milk cows.

There was also a mean old Black Angus bull that I had to tread very carefully around. Sometimes I would try to hurry up the old Black Angus bull and he would spin around and attack old Blackie and me. Blackie, of course, had no trouble jumping out of his way but I really had to grab onto old Blackie's mane so as not to fall off as I was riding bareback. If I had ever fallen off in front of that old bull I'm sure he would have trampled me into the ground. But, of course, I had no fear of that because I knew old Blackie would never let me fall off.

Sure, there were times when I did fall off Blackie. Fortunately, that mean old bull was never around when that happened. That was always very humiliating because invariably this would happen when I was out in the middle of the 640 acre pasture and the closest fence post was a half mile away. I would have to lead Blackie by the reins to the closest fence so I could climb a fence post and then stand on top of this fence post and ask old Blackie to come alongside so that I could jump onto his back. And, of course, old Blackie was always happy to oblige. Now, of course, I always figured I was the best darn cowboy in the country, which might have been true because all the other cowboys had gone overseas to fight in the war. But Mr. Rash could see that old Blackie was looking out for me as Blackie always walked as if he was walking on egg shells so as not to let his tenderfoot cowboy fall off.

So it was that Mr. Rash thought that with a good horse like Blackie I might be able to keep the cows out of the oat field. Now this was the war years, you remember, and everything was rationed. But the government still expected the farmers to give their maximum effort to help with the war effort. So Mr. Rash ploughed up eighty acres of pasture up on the flat land, as the cattle usually stayed down in the river valley where the grass was nice and green. Now there was one problem. Barbed wire was a restricted item and very hard to get, so Mr. Rash could not build a fence to keep the cattle out of his oat field. So if old Blackie and I could keep them cows out of that field we would be helping the war effort. Wow! Just think—old Blackie and I helping with the war effort!

So Mr. Rash showed me how to build a tent. But he didn't have time to do it for me, so he just rolled up some long poles into an old tarpaulin, and he hand-ed them to me as I sat on old Blackie's back, and away I went to set up camp on the hilltop to watch over them cows. Wow! Was this ever exciting! Mother even packed me a lunch and gave me a bottle of orangeade to drink. Now this was pret-ty special because you only got orangeade on special occasions. Mother bought the orangeade from the Raleigh man who came around about every three months, so we had to make it last until he came again.

But, of course, when I was sitting in the tent drinking my orangeade Blackie would have his head inside the tent, so I would have to share my orangeade with him. I poured some into my hand and let him lick it out of my hand. Blackie and I really liked that orangeade, so we had to make several trips back to the house to get more. Mother reminded me that when it was gone there would be no more until the Raleigh man came again. But, golly, how could a cowboy not share his orangeade with his horse?

One day when I returned to my tent from getting another supply of orangeade, there were those dang cows in the oat field. Gee whiz! I had better get them outta there or I was liable to lose my job. Well, as hard as I tried, there was no way I could chase them cows outta that oat field. In fact, it looked like them cows were laughing at me because they knew that I was just a kid and didn't know how to chase cows. Well, that just made me burn so I said, "Okay, Blackie, you go gettem!"

Wellsir, you just wouldn't believe what happened next. Old Blackie charged them and bit them on the rump. He was just waiting for me to give him the go-ahead and, boy, did he ever get after them cows. All I had to do was hang onto his mane as he did all the work, and when he bit them on the rump, boys, you should have seen them cows jump. It didn't take Blackie long to get them cows outta the oat field 'cause now the cows knew Blackie was in charge and the kid was just along for the ride.

Well, that night when I come in for supper I told old Mr. Rash what a smart horse Blackie was. Mr. Rash seemed quite surprised because he never figured old Blackie was good for much except for kids to ride. Whenever Mr. Rash hitched Blackie into a harness to pull a wagon or hay mower, Blackie wouldn't pull worth a darn, so the farmer didn't bother with him much. Of course, I thought Blackie was the greatest horse in the world and I would spend the whole day just sitting on his back watching them sneaky old cows who wanted to get into the oat field, or just lie on his back and watch the clouds drift by.

When I came into the house at night, Mr. Rash would order me away from the table because I stunk just like a horse from all his sweat that had soaked into my jeans during the day. My mother would have to rush me into the bathroom and give me a quick bath and a change of clothes before I could eat supper. I never thought I stunk. I thought old Blackie smelled wonderful.

Blackie was my best friend and only companion while I did my job keeping after them cows. He knew there were no fence posts near the tent site on the hilltop. The closest fence post was a half mile away. That was no way for a cowboy to herd cattle. So I had to bring an orange crate out from the house to stand on. Blackie waited patiently while I got on the orange crate and straddled his back.

Now, Mr. Rash thought that I was doing a very good job, and so for a bonus he made me a slingshot because any self-respecting cowboy should have a slingshot. But I was also given strict orders not to shoot out any windows. Hey! I would never dream of doing a thing like that. As my dad was always away, Mr. Rash and I got very close and he was the only male influence I had. I prized my slingshot that he had given me more than anything. After that, I always carried a pocket full of pebbles that I could shoot at a gopher or at an ornery cow. I was always on the lookout for some nice smooth round pebbles for my slingshot.

One day as I was riding across the valley, I saw something glinting in the sunlight. When I went to investigate the source of this reflection I discovered it was a black flint arrowhead. Down in the bottom of the river valley there were many large holes dug into the ground by the ancient buffaloes as they pawed the ground to dust themselves to keep the flies away. Some of these holes were big enough for Mr. Rash to back his truck into and load cattle. I jumped down from Blackie's back and picked up the arrowhead. As I felt the smooth, sharp arrowhead in my hand, I could imagine the Indian that might have had it and how he might have used it to hunt the buffalo so many years ago. When I showed the arrowhead to Mr. Rash, he was surprised to see it, as he had never found one. Poor Mr. Rash was always so busy he didn't have time to look for arrowheads.

Blackie and I were doing our job helping with the war effort, but I thought we could do better. I decided I had to learn how to put that big western saddle onto Blackie's back so I could mount him quicker and stay steady on him while we were out herding. The saddle weighed as much as I did, and Blackie's back was higher than I could reach, but I was not deterred. I knocked the saddle off the rail where it sat and dragged it over to Blackie's side, then tied a rope to one of the stirrups and threw the other end of the rope over Blackie's back. Then I grabbed hold of the other end of the rope and pulled as hard as I could. But I couldn't get that stirrup to come over Blackie's back. The poor old horse winced with pain because every time I pulled on the rope it cut into his back. I doubled my efforts so I could get it right and save him from hurting. I was sweating and fuming when I heard a voice.

"Can I help you with that saddle?"

There was the man I had been missing for almost a year. He was dressed in a navy officer's uniform; the most handsome man I had ever seen. I wasn't too old to cry as I rushed to my father's strong arms. He held me as I breathed in the scent of the faraway places and the big ships and the war effort that had soaked into his clothes. I cried tears, but I was bursting with happiness, and then my dad said, "This is a pretty good looking horse you have here. Let's see what he can do."

Dad took off his hat and coat and adjusted the saddle properly before jumping on old Blackie's back. He rode him around the yard and soon Blackie was galloping. Then Dad jumped off Blackie's back and, grasping the saddle horn only, he swung down to graze the ground and just as quickly swooped right back onto Blackie's back and swung down to the other side and back again. The poor old horse didn't know what to make of all this, as it was the first time he had a trick rider in the saddle. The sensible horse figured Dad was out of control and falling off, so he kept stopping. I watched as Dad galloped Blackie at a full gallop doing a handstand in the saddle. I never knew my father could do anything like this. I had never seen anything like it. This was a great homecoming—my dad so handsome and strong and skillful. I wanted to be with my dad every minute.

All too soon he had to go back to Halifax to board another ship. I didn't see my dad again until the spring of 1946 when he was honourably discharged from the navy.

The days were long and lonely after Dad left. I remembered with awe how he first rode Blackie and I thought I would do some tricks with Blackie too. I tied Blackie's long tail to the tongue of my little red wagon with some binder twine so I could give my sister a ride—because she was always bugging me about riding Blackie. We sat in the wagon and I told Blackie to *gittup*. I didn't have any reins long enough to steer him, so Blackie just started to walk back to the barn. The barn was situated at the bottom of a slope, so on the way to the barn the wagon tongue kept running into Blackie's heels. An ordinary horse would have kicked our heads off but not old Blackie. He just stood there. I had no idea of what hardship I was putting on my dear old pal.

"It's okay, Blackie, a few more steps and we will be on level ground," I coaxed.

But we never reached level ground. Mr. Rash appeared from out of nowhere and gently took hold of Blackie's halter and told us kids to get out of the wagon. The way he said it real quiet I knew we were in trouble. Mr. Rash cut the wagon tongue loose of Blackie's tail with his pocket knife.

"Get to the house while I put Blackie in the barn."

Now my sister was squealing, "I told you it was a bad idea."

Oh sure, now she turns against me, I thought. See if I ever give her a ride again.

I went in the house and sat in a wooden chair at the kitchen table wishing I could die.

"What's the matter?" my mother eyed me.

"Nothin'."

My sister opened her big mouth and blurted, "He tied his wagon to Blackie's tail and the wagon ran into Blackie's heels and we nearly got killed."

"We did not," I protested. "Blackie would never hurt us."

And then, Mr. Rash was striding through the wooden screen door and the lines on his face made him fierce and scary at the same time.

"Margaret!" he exclaimed to my mother but he glared at me. "Do you know what that idiotic kid of yours did? It's a wonder to me that he's still alive. Never have I seen a horse endure such abuse and not retaliate. That poor horse was a wreck. Standing stiff and shaking with the sweat pouring off him, but he wouldn't kick when the wagon tongue hit his heels. I would like to whip the tar out of your son but I know he's too young. So the worst thing I can think of is to restrict him to his room for three days."

"Can't I even go tell Blackie that I'm sorry?" I pleaded.

"Yes, you can—in three days' time!"

Now my mother said, "You go take a bath, and go to your bed without any supper, and pray to God for forgiveness, and bless that dear Blackie for not kicking your brains out."

The next three days were the worst of my life. I had to stay in my room and study my school book. I hated school and studying school books was probably the worst thing Mother could have made me do. I would rather have had Mr. Rash whip the tar out of me. To make things worse, old Blackie was out at the corral gate whinnying for me to come and play. But I could not because Mr. Rash was a man of his word, so there was no need to ask if I could go out and play. At least old Blackie had forgiven me and was ready to go riding again. Oh, how could a cowboy not lay down his life for a friend like that?

When my three days of punishment had been served, I could hardly eat my breakfast fast enough so I could run out to see my dearest friend. I nearly flew up the railings to reach my arms round good old Blackie's sturdy neck. Old Blackie and I had a great time riding all over the ranch that day, but after that Mr. Rash didn't seem too friendly towards me.

Well, when the summer was over and it seemed that Mr. Rash didn't need any help for the winter, Mother and sister and I moved on to another job at a sheep ranch. I was heartbroken. I tearfully said goodbye to my dearest friend. Old Blackie seemed to know I was leaving as he hung his head over the corral gate and I petted his nose and bid him farewell.

About a month or so after we left Mr. Rash's ranch, Mother got a letter from him saying would she "please come back to work for him because old Blackie does nothing but whimper and cry for that boy to come and ride him again. He mopes around the corral all day waiting for that kid and won't eat anything, and then he wanders out to that little tent on the hilltop with his head hanging down. Margaret, you've got to bring that boy back here before that old horse dies of a broken heart."

I begged Mother to go back to Mr. Rash's ranch, but she said she just couldn't just leave her new job and so I never saw old Blackie again.

When my mother saw how much I missed old Blackie she sewed me a doll that looked just like him. I kept it for many years, but then one day a little boy saw it and fell in love with it, so I gave it to him to keep because I had my memories of old Blackie to cherish.

WHEN THE SKY GOT BIGGER

Lana Skauge

"You're heading for the prairies."

He loved the sound of those words—*the prairies*.

"Make sure you pack for all kinds of weather. You never know."

"Mom, I know, I know. It was freezing last time. Then it turned wicked hot."

"What if you get bored? Are you sure you can handle the small town scene that long?"

"I can take it."

"I couldn't get out of there fast enough when I was a kid. After high school I saved my money for a train ticket and got out of there."

"I wish *I* could take the train."

"It doesn't run there anymore, honey."

The boy's parents fussed over him as they pulled up to the Greyhound bus depot. He hated that.

"We love you," he heard his dad call out and hoped that no one else had heard.

He climbed aboard the bus and plunked into the front seat. He leaned his head to watch his parents disappear through the automatic, sliding glass doors of the bus station.

"Goin' solo, eh?" said the driver. "Best way to travel. Just you and the road."

"Yeah," spoke the boy. "Best way to travel. Just me and the road."

He felt his own words drop into the pit of his stomach. He wished his parents were sitting beside him now. The boy stared out the wide window and watched the city disappear into a long ribbon of highway, wheat fields, summer fallow, and the sky—bigger than anything, bright blue with clouds drifting. The longer he gazed the more his thoughts drifted too. Not to anywhere in particular, just away. He hugged his backpack with his treats and allowance inside and leaned his forehead onto the cool surface of glass. He couldn't help but let his eyes get lazy with the light and soon he fell asleep.

The brakes squealed to a halt. The dust billowed over the sidewalk. The boy's eyes opened.

"Clarksville!" announced the driver.

The boy managed his way out of the bus and saw immediately that he was there waiting.

"Hey, sport. Yer mother pack ya a three course meal in that bag?"

"Hi Grandpa! Yeah, and she made me bring my parka!"

"Good! You can sleep outside by the shed then."

The boy grinned. The teasing had begun. Grandpa took his keys and opened the driver's side to the old Ford truck. He handed them to the boy.

"Go ahead. Hop in."

"You want me to start it up or somethin'?"

"Heck no, boy. I want you to drive."

"Grandpa, I am only eleven and a half years old."

"Look more like a teenager to me. Go ahead. Drive."

The boy was scared stiff. He had the keys in his hand but his feet were stuck to the ground and his head hung down to stare at the tops of his scuffed runners. Grandpa let loose with a laugh.

"I was just jokin'. You worry too much. You're just like your mother. Now move over before you have yourself a heart attack."

Grandpa started up the truck and decided to take the long way home. It was about a three minute longer drive. Clarksville was a small prairie town with a few paved streets, not many folks left to call it home, and wheat fields surrounding it on every side. Grandpa pulled over and got out of the truck to stretch. The boy jumped out of the truck too. A sea of waist-high purple flax waved about them. They walked through it. Grandpa pointed back to the grain elevator that stood like a sentinel in the big sky.

"He'll be comin' down soon."

"What, Grandpa? The grain elevator?"

"Yep, he's old like me. People don't like old. They want somethin' bigger and better. I remember when that grain elevator was built. The train would load up with wheat from that elevator and take off and feed a world. Made us feel kinda special, us being able to feed the world. Now the train is gone and the grain elevator's days are numbered."

The boy and his grandpa stood in the field among the sway of flax and the wind picked up from behind them. They turned to see dark violet clouds roll in.

"Some things you just don't see comin'," the old man spoke softly. The boy saw his Grandpa's face change and he felt uncomfortable.

"Grandpa, you okay?"

Grandpa shuffled his feet and cleared his throat.

"Some things you just don't see comin'—like the weather. It can change in a minute. Don't worry, boy, there's no snow in these clouds, probably just thunderheads. Let's go now. Grandma's waiting."

They pulled up to a little white house bordered with brightly painted petunias. The screen door flew open and Grandma wrapped herself around the boy. She was the only woman allowed to hug him in public.

"Look at you!" She stepped back to observe the full height of the boy. "You look old enough to drive."

"Grandma!" the boy blushed.

"What's the matter honey? Your Grandpa scare you?"

The old fellow grinned as he sat down at the kitchen table.

He took off his John Deere cap and the boy noticed his white forehead.

"That there is called a farmer's tan. Sign of a good, honest, hard-workin' man."

Grandma served the dinner—hot roast beef, peas and carrots from the garden, mashed potatoes, and thick, delicious gravy ladled over everything.

Bang! A crash of thunder interrupted the clinking of the boy's fork on the sturdy china plate. Grandma ran to the kitchen window and inspected the sky.

"Don't worry, Mother. Probably just thunderheads."

The hail came down in buckets, pelting the roof and pattering on the windows. The storm was over in minutes. The old woman went out on to the veranda and surveyed the damage. She walked to the shed and the boy could see her back was stooped and he thought how she was getting older. His thoughts brightened when she came back with her arms full of petunias.

"Not this year, mother nature. I have lived here over fifty years and I'll be darned if one prairie storm is going to ruin my day. Come on, boy, we've got some replanting to do."

"Grandma, what if it starts storming again?"

"Don't worry, honey. I've got more petunias in the shed."

They got down on their knees on the slick wet grass that had gotten greener in the storm and replanted petunias amidst the white icy sludge.

That night the boy dreamed of dusty roads on the wide open prairie and tall grain elevators, a storm in the distance.

In the morning Grandpa and the boy piled into the old Ford truck and drove to the grain elevator. When they arrived Grandpa warned the boy, "You gotta be careful. It's not for play now. This old fellow has been abandoned and he's in poor repair."

The boy placed each foot carefully as he stepped. He stayed close to his grandpa. A choking scent of grain dust and prairie dirt was coming off the wooden walls.

"Watch out for that pit. You wouldn't want to fall in there," Grandpa explained.

"What's it for?"

"My Dad and I would drive our grain truck right into this here elevator, see? The elevator operator would open up a chute in the back and test the grain. If it was a good crop my dad made good money and if it wasn't . . . . Anyways, Dad

would get paid and then the grain would be stored right here until the train came to take it away."

Grandpa looked down at the pit and his face changed again.

"Look at that!" he snorted. "There's enough grain there to feed a whole family. What a waste."

The old man stood and stared for a long time.

"Grandpa, are you okay?"

"Too many memories, boy. Old people are full of them."

The boy followed his grandpa out of the old elevator, and the two crossed the field without speaking. The boy knew they were headed for the tall poplar tree where Grandpa liked to rest. Grandpa leaned on the rough barked trunk and eased himself down slowly. He sat on the earth with his back supported by the tree. He placed a canvas pack on his bent knees.

"Let's see what kind of treats Grandma's packed."

The summer sun was high in the sky. The sky was clear and blue, and the quiet magnified the buzzing of flies. They shared sandwiches and pickles that Grandma had wrapped carefully in waxed paper. Grandpa fell asleep as he always did after a meal. The boy gazed at the fields of grain and saw how the breeze moved over the grain like the wind on the sea. He turned his eyes toward Main Street. All the stores were boarded up now. Everything was quiet. It was like looking at an old postcard—hardly real. He lifted his eyes to the grain elevator, tall and still. Halfway up its wooden face the painted letters of *Clarksville* were peeling off. Soon, you wouldn't even know what town you passed through. The boy looked over at his grandpa whose knees were slouching sideways and whose breath was coming in deep rumbles.

The boy stood to stretch, and the urge to take one more look at the old elevator propelled his boy's limbs forward. He ran back through the field to the great creaking door of the old elevator and peered inside. Quickly it slammed behind him. The lights went out. The scent no longer stung in his nostrils but hung heavy like a blanket. *It smells different in the dark,* he thought, and the image of the pit that Grandpa had shown him earlier loomed in his mind. He prayed that he wouldn't find it.

"Hey, you okay?" came a voice in the dark

The lights went on, and the boy saw a figure dressed in strange clothes leaning by the switch.

"Oops! Sorry about that."

The boy thought this fellow looked weird—like he'd popped out of a museum.

"I look pretty funny, eh? Your grandpa probably wore clothes like this. These here are knickers and these things holding up my pants are suspenders," chuckled the young man.

"You know my grandpa?" the boy asked, catching his breath and fixing his eyes on the stranger.

"I figure he's the old guy who likes to sleep under that poplar. Hey, my name's Jake. We shouldn't be in here, you know. It's not safe. I could show you something else though. Do you want to see something else?"

"I don't know. I'm supposed to stay with my grandpa," said the boy.

"I could take you to the slough nearby. It's just behind where he's napping. We can keep him in sight."

"Okay, let's go. It's creepy in here," said the boy.

They walked hurriedly past the sleeping grandpa and broke into a run near the slough. Cattails sprang from the marshy land and red-winged blackbirds called out warnings. Frogs, tadpoles, garter snakes, and mud begged to be closely examined. A slough was a prairie kid's paradise. When the boy noticed his grandpa standing beneath the poplar and surveying the fields, he knew it was time to go.

"Hey, my grandpa's going to wonder where I am."

Jake extended his hand. "Here. You can have this."

The boy felt the cold smooth weight of something in his hand. His face lit up when he saw that the object was a penknife.

"I'll see you later."

Before the boy could say much, Grandpa was calling.

That evening they sat on the porch and looked out on the prairie as Grandma quizzed them about their day's adventure.

"Well, dear, did he fall asleep?" Grandma smiled.

"Now, Mother," Grandpa defended himself as the boy nodded, and they all laughed.

"Grandpa," the boy spoke hesitantly, "I went back to the elevator while you were sleeping. There was a guy there. Look what he gave me."

The boy reached into his pocket and pulled out the penknife. When he told Grandpa the stranger's name, the old man became uneasy. Grandma took the knife and examined it.

"Well, Grandpa, it has your name on it and the date 1922."

Grandpa wiped his large rough hand over his face and shifted his weight in his chair. He leaned forward and peered at a figure coming up the road wearing knicker pants and suspenders. He slumped back in his chair looking like he'd seen a ghost. Grandma noticed the approaching figure that had startled her husband, and she stifled a cry with a hand to her mouth.

"Grandma, what is it?"

"Oh, it's this prairie heat. Wheat fields look like lakes . . . trees look like people . . ."

The boy watched the figure get closer.

"Jake! It's Jake!"

"The only Jake I know died three years ago. He was an old man and I gave him that penknife when we were kids. He was my best friend."

The boy noticed the lines on Grandpa's face and how his cheeks were sucked in. The old man spoke to the stranger in a voice that sounded too brave. "Who are you?"

Jake took off his cap. "Sir, I'm Jake Junior, the grandson."

"He thought you were a ghost, dear!" Grandma laughed and breathed deep.

"But why do you wear those old clothes?" Grandpa inquired.

"I found them in a trunk at the farmhouse. Grandma says she likes to see me in these old things. It reminds her of him."

"Well, you look just like him," Grandpa said in an easier tone, resting back into his chair. "Come and sit down and have some lemonade." Then, turning to the old woman who was already going through the screen door to her kitchen, "Mother, get this young Jake some lemonade."

The remainder of the boy's prairie visit was spent with Grandpa and Jake. Sometimes they drove for miles in the old truck leaving a plume of dust behind them and going nowhere. On many afternoons the boys mucked about the slough while grandpa napped beneath the poplar. Always they returned to the little white house and Grandma piling on potatoes and pouring more gravy. The summer days stretched long and slipped by quickly.

On the last night of his visit the boy was awakened.

"Fire! Fire on Main Street!" a voice called in the night.

Grandpa started up the Ford and they got in, wearing jackets over their pajamas. The sky above the town glowed red. The grain elevator blazed like a huge warning flare. A crowd of people had gathered. The volunteer fire crew realized it was hopeless to try to contain the raging flames. Their job was to keep the crowd back a safe distance.

Grandpa called out, "Let it burn. He's had his day. Let him burn!"

A strange silence fell over the crowd. Grandpa's eyes swept around the throng of onlookers and he looked at each one in turn as he spoke.

"You see, when the farmer dropped off his grain and got paid he didn't go to the city. If he needed the dentist, there was one around the corner. Maybe he'd mail some letters. Post office? It was just beside the dentist. The general store was down the street. Saturday night there'd be a dance at the community hall. The grain elevator gave this town a reason for being here. We all know this town's had its day. We have to face it. We have to let him burn."

They watched the elevator burn that night. Flames shot up and died down to flare up again with a change in the wind. Black smoke filled the black night. Eventually people straggled home to their beds, leaving the firefighters to observe the scene.

The boy tossed in his sleep, and in the morning he dragged his exhausted body out of bed. His bag, which had been packed the day before, sat ready on the red patterned linoleum. Breakfast was oatmeal eaten in silence. When he finished, he rinsed his bowl and spoon and set them on a tea towel. Then, they must head to the bus depot. They drove the long way through town, past the empty stores, past the poplar tree and the slough, past the place where the grain elevator used to stand.

"Look!" said the boy, "the sky got bigger."

Grandpa pulled the truck over to the side of the road. They sat and stared at the empty space where the elevator had been, where fallen debris now smouldered. It was clear that new space had been created. The town of Clarksville had been changed.

The boy sat between his grandpa and grandma on the grey bench seat in the Ford. He had thought the sky was the biggest thing he could ever know. Now he saw that it was greater than that. He knew there was something bigger than the grain elevator, bigger than the prairie, bigger even than the sky.

LET THE FUR FLY

SHOWDOWN AT ED'S BAKERY

Lodgepole (sometimes also known as Michael Ebsworth)

"Now you talk about stories—how it used to be out here on the prairie. I got some I could tell you about when the elevators stood tall against the sky. Why, you could pretty near recognize any town by the signature it wrote on the skyline! You know, I even remember once I went whistlin' right past the town I was headed for. They tore the elevator down since I was last there, and I was gone by before I even knew I was coming in."

Lodgepole—you know, I don't think any of us ever knew his real name, if he had one, that is—stretched, put his feet, complete with two layers of heavy grey work socks, a little nearer to the fire, reached out for another cup of coffee.

"But I was fixin' to tell you about some of the folks that lived here in Prickly Pear years back," he said. He took a good slug from the coffee cup, topped up the mug with a big shot of rye, and eased back in his chair—getting comfortable, getting ready.

"Did I ever tell you," he asked, "about Homer over at the car wash and his feud with Ed at the Bake Shop? No? Well, they were about as fine a pair of characters as you could find in any town, anywhere.

"Come to think of it, we had a lot of characters in Prickly Pear . . ." He took another slug of his strong coffee—downright muscular now, with all that rye— and stretched nearer to the fire's warmth. Frost painted the windows. The cold norther whistled in the chimney, smoke flying out on the wind and sweeping down across the windowpanes. He shivered a moment. "Bad night to be lost out there! In fact, I remember once when . . .

"But I started to tell you about Homer and Ed, didn't I? That other story'll keep awhile.

"Back before they got that brushless car-wash thing down at the Wild Rose service station, we had a coin-op car wash over there at the corner of Railway and Rattler Street. 'Course, before that we had actual people who washed cars—at least for those as was too lazy to do their own. Anyway, back to what I was tellin' you. That coin-op car wash—the Apollo, I think they called it, to make you think the space age had come to Prickly Pear, as if we didn't have space enough out here already . . . but I'm wandering off again, I guess. Homer Johnson, he owned that coin-op wash.

"The Apollo car wash—think of that! Mighty impressive, with a pressure pump and a stream of water that'd knock you right on your overcoat, if you know the old rhyme. But it was really just a single stall car wash. You fed coins into a box on the wall. It counted up how much you were willin' to spend and gave you so many minutes of high-pressure water. You could soap and rinse and even wax. An' some of those guys, you know, they spent more in there on their cars than they'd spend takin' their best girl to dinner and a movie. Which reminds me of some great nights down there at the Bijou . . .

"What? . . . Oh, yeah. I was going to tell you about Homer and the feud he had with Ed. Sorry. There's just so many stories about those times in Prickly Pear that I sometimes don't remember which one I was telling.

"Like I said, Homer Johnson had that single stall car wash. Each day, he'd take out a key, open up the coin box, and spill out all its contents into a canvas bag from the Prickly Pear Credit. I remember one time, there was a fellow named Clyde was managing the Credit. Now there's a story . . .

"Yeah! Yeah! I'll tell you about Homer. Don't get things in a knot! Tellin' a story out here is kind of like trailin' cows on a horse. You have to go up, over, and maybe around a few hills an' ride pretty deep in the brush before you find some of 'em.

"Like I said, each day Homer'd open up the coin box in the car wash. He'd take the bag of coins into a little lean-to shed on the side of the wash—he called it his office. Some office! An old kitchen table, a chair with the stuffing mostly out, and barely room to squeak between the two. And a little back room, too. The door said *STALLIONS OR FILLIES—IF YOU DON'T WANNA MINGLE, LOCK THE DOOR!* As if anyone'd wanna mingle in there, if you take my meaning. More like you wouldn't wanna actually put anything down in there.

"Yeah! Yeah! I'll tell it. You just give it time to stretch out. That's how it was in Prickly Pear. Still should be, if you ask me. You all want everything in 30-second TV bites nowadays.

"Anyways . . . Homer, he loved those coins. And he loved his account down there at the Credit. Leastways, he did until that time that Clyde . . . but I'll save that for another day. Homer loved money. He loved the sound of it. He loved the smell of it. He loved to see the numbers growing in his bankbook. The more the better. He even liked all the things that could be bought with the money. Just one thing he didn't like. And that was actually having to spend the money, having to put down the asking price for anything at all.

"Down the street, over there at the corner of Main and Rattler, where they built that new courthouse a few years back, there was a bakery. For a few years there, before the spot was bought—stolen, more like, government expropriations bein' like they are—it was called the Copenhagen Bakery and Cafe. But back then, it was just Ed's Bake Shop. It was started back a long time ago by Ed Larsen. And it was a plain spot. Mixers and bake ovens at the back, a couple of scrubbed wood tables up front, so you could have a coffee and spin a line or two with Ed.

"Now Ed, there was a great guy! You know how some bakeries have stuff out in the window, and you walk up and see it, and it looks so good, maybe smells so good, too. And you think, that's just got to be so good. I better have me one of those. So you buy it, and you take it out, and you bite into it—and you find you could've got a better grade of sawdust down at the Beaver-Bite Lumber. But Ed Larsen could bake! If it looked good, smelled good, then you better buy it, 'cause it'd always taste even better. And now, what with progress an' all, machines and robot automation makin' the bread, you can buy that baked shave-cream from McGillicuddy's up there in the city. Some call it bread, I guess . . .

"Anyhow, like I was saying, Ed Larsen could really bake. And at the end of every day, he had a good bit of money to take down to the Credit. That reminds of the time when Clyde . . . but that'll do for another time as well.

"How 'bout another mug of that coffee? A hit from the rye bottle wouldn't go too far amiss, either.

"Thanks. Now back to the feud between Homer and Ed.

"Those two – you know, they were about as different as two men could be. Ed, he was always really trim. Clean, well dressed. Immaculate, as the big-city folks might say, and dapper, as my grandma and my ma did say. But I guess he had to be. You probably want to buy your baked goods from someone who's clean, don't you? And Homer? Well, since he didn't have to wash the cars, just see to the soap an' maintain the pump an' tend to the coin box, like I said, he lived a kind of idle life. Anytime the weather was good enough, you'd find him outside in the street with a couple of hubcaps set up about the distance of a horseshoe pitch. And he'd be tryin' to get a bet goin' with anyone who passed by, tryin' to sucker them into pitchin' washers with him. That was a mug's game, if ever there was. And if the weather wasn't so good, you'd find Homer indoors in his garage next door to the car wash, an' he'd be up to his elbows in the guts of some old car that he thought was the latest wonder of the world. So, between the road dust and the grease, Homer was a pretty murky sight to have on your horizon.

"Still, Homer and Ed were alike in one way at least. They both loved their money, hated to part with it, and were always looking for some way to get more of it.

"Like I told you, Ed's bread and buns and cookies looked good, smelled great, and tasted even better. And if the wind was just right, the scent of the bakery would drift down the block to the car wash, and next thing you know, out the door'd come Homer like a hound on the scent of a ripe gopher. He'd drift up outside the bakery door, lean on the signpost at the corner of the street an' just stand there. I swear, you could see his nostrils flare just to get more of that wonderful scent off the bread an' all. But Homer being so scruffy an' dirty an' all that, he kind of put off some of Ed's more refined customers. An' besides that, Ed had this feeling that Homer was out there getting something for nothing, an' that went against his grain for sure. But I don't think for awhile that Ed really understood what

Homer was doing there. He lived in the scent of the bakery all the time, so it wasn't anything special to him.

"What I do know is that Ed really hated seeing Homer out there day after day, lounging against the corner sign and clogging up the sidewalk. So one day impatience and curiosity got the better of him. He dusted off his hands and went . . . kinda brisk, like . . . out the door.

"'Homer,' he says, 'what you do 'ere outside my door ever' day? You come all times, stand 'ere, stare in my windows. You put off my customers, wreck my business! What you do here?'

"'Now, Ed!' says Homer, 'you got no cause to complain. I'm just here enjoyin' the prairie air. After all, we got so much of it, don't we? I will say, though, it smells better here than most anywhere else I can think of.'

"So Ed thinks to himself that Homer's out to get something for nothing, as if that'd be any kind of surprise. And he decides that he'll either get rid of Homer or get something out of it himself. He says, 'Homer, I don' want that you come 'ere any more. You clog up the sidewalk and put off my customers.'

"But Homer says—like so many freeloaders do, maybe—'It's a free country, an' free prairie air, an' I'll come stand here just however often I want.'

"So Ed thinks about this a bit more. Then he says, 'Well, Homer, you're right. It is a free country. And the air is free, too. But I bake to sell an' I know you come here to smell my baking. So you enjoy the free country all you want, the free prairie air, too. But if you want to smell my baking, you pay. Ever' time you come to smell my baking you pay me fifty cents. You pay, you enjoy it all you want!'

"Now I have to tell you that Homer really didn't like that very much. Still, a hustler knows a hustler, and he knew when he was beat. An' he looks at Ed an' says, 'You win!' An' muttering things like 'cheapskate' an' worse, he takes off down the street.

"Ed was amazed. He never thought to win so easy. He slapped his hands together—that's that!—and went back into the bakery.

"But, you know, that Homer was never one to be beat too easy. He was always figuring how he could come out on top of anything that came along. So he was thinking hard as he walked back to the car wash. An' just as he was going in the door, he knew what to do.

"How about a little more coffee? Yeah, that's great, thanks! Did I ever tell you about when Clyde came to manage the Credit? Oh, finish the story about the feud—Homer and Ed? Okay! Like I said, don't get everything in a knot.

"Homer walks into the car wash. He goes over to the wall where the coin box is, an' he takes a tire iron an' rips the coin box right off the wall. Then he grabs one of those hubcaps he uses for pitchin' washers, dumps out the washers an' dirt, an' he shakes all the money out of the coin box into the hubcap. Then he storms out the car wash door an' back up the street to the bakery. He leans up against the street corner sign, fastens his eyes on the best of the baked stuff in the window— that stare would've put off a stampeding buffalo—flares out his nostrils real wide to sniff those good smells comin' like always from the bakery. An' all the while, he's shakin' that hubcap full of money so as to make a din to wake the sleepers up there on the hill of stones.

"Out in back of the bakery, Ed hears the noise—thinks maybe someone's dropped a muffler or broke a spring on their truck. But when he comes t'look, all he sees is Homer, standing right where he always does, but now Homer's shakin' the hubcap for all he's wort—an' that was a fair bit, at least until Clyde . . .

"Okay! Okay! We're gettin' there. No need to get excited. After all, I never do . . .

"Like I was saying, Ed sees—an' hears—Homer out there, jus' where he never wanted to see him again. He says—kinda agitated, like—'Homer! What you do back here? I tol' you I don' wan' you 'ere out front my bakery! You sniff, you pay!'

"An' Homer says, 'Why, Ed, that's jus' what I'm doin'! I'm payin' for the smell of your baking with the sound of my money!'"

THE BEAR

M. Jennie Frost

One fine morning in early August around the year 1900, Mrs. Wheatley called on Netta Shulstad and suggested they go raspberry picking out at the Hendersons' farm. Seventeen-year-old Netta thought it was a wonderful idea. Her mother had another day of bean picking and canning lined up for her. Netta had picked and ended beans yesterday, and picked and shelled peas the day before. She wasn't looking forward to more of the same. Mind you, raspberries didn't seem more exciting. Worse, actually; Netta hated picking raspberries. But at least there would be a long wagon ride in the sunshine and Mrs. Wheatley was such fun.

Mrs. Wheatley was a young widow who lived near the Shulstads in Strathcona. In 1900, all the part of Edmonton south of the Saskatchewan River was still a separate town called Strathcona. No one knew anything about Mr. Wheatley. Mrs. Wheatley never mentioned him. He was a bit of a mystery, a subject for speculation. But everyone knew and enjoyed the company of Mrs. Wheatley. She was older than Netta, about twenty-five, and always friendly and lively. A day with her, even if it included picking raspberries, was bound to be a good day.

Netta rushed to get permission from her mother to go with Mrs. Wheatley to the Hendersons' farm. Mrs. Shulstad weighed the merits of finishing the beans against the prospect of eating fresh berries and let Netta go. The two young women were soon in Mrs. Wheatley's wagon heading out of town.

You may know the round barn and old farmhouse from the Henderson farm now preserved as part of the museum buildings in Fort Edmonton Park. When I was a child, those buildings were still on their original site at what was then the southwest edge of Edmonton. They were abandoned when I saw them, so weathered that their shingle siding was a dark grey-brown like an elm tree's trunk. I watched for those buildings eagerly when we drove that way. Passing them meant we were out of the city and into the country.

When Netta and Mrs. Wheatley set off for that same farm, it was a long way out in the country, far from their houses at the edge of Strathcona. Getting to the Hendersons' farm meant a long wagon ride over dusty, bumpy roads, but Netta thoroughly enjoyed that drive through the August countryside. The goldenrod and asters bloomed yellow and purple in the ditches, and in the fields on either side the yellow-green of plumy barley made a pleasing contrast to the grey-green of feathery oats.

When they reached the Hendersons' neat white frame house set by the unusual round barn, they stopped to speak with Mr. Henderson. "Good morning, Mrs. Wheatley, Miss Shulstad!" Mr. Henderson called as he came down from his covered veranda. He smiled at both women but he walked to Mrs. Wheatley's side of the wagon to talk. "Of course you may pick raspberries, as many as you like. They grow thickest at the western edge of the pasture down that track there, the field just above the river. Why don't you shut the gate when you go in? Then you can turn your horse loose to graze while you're picking berries."

Mrs. Wheatley thanked Mr. Henderson and drove the wagon down the track. She pulled up at the edge of the pasture and unhitched her horse while Netta shut the gate. As the two women crossed the pasture to the clumps of wild raspberry bushes on the other side, Mrs. Wheatley commented, "How pleasantly Mr. Henderson welcomed us. He's very hospitable, isn't he?"

"Yes" Netta agreed, "and aren't the Hendersons generous to share their berries with anyone who wants to pick them?"

They set to work picking the delicate berries from the canes. As Netta had anticipated, picking those berries wasn't much fun. They were wild bushes, so she had to bend over low to pick the berries and the footing around the bushes wasn't clear. The bushes were all mixed up with wild rosebushes, thistles, and last year's dead canes, so the going was very prickly and tangled. The bushes tore at her long skirts and snagged her stockings. The hot sun beat down on her and there was no wind. When Netta stood straight to ease her aching back and wipe the sweat from her face, she wondered why she'd wanted to come, but then she sampled the juicy fruit and remembered. Then, too, Mrs. Wheatley was telling her about a church social that Netta had missed last Saturday. Her comments on the people who'd attended kept Netta giggling and prompted her to share her own observations about people in the congregation. The two women had to call to each other from their respective bushes—they were fairly widely separated—but the banter they shared kept Netta going.

When Netta's bucket was three-quarters full she spied a particularly bountiful bush. Unfortunately, that bush wasn't easily accessible. How was she going to get in there? Perhaps if she first swung her pail over and set it down, she'd have both hands free to get around the vicious tangle of rosebushes and thistles to approach the berry bush from behind. Netta got her pail safely in place and set out to break her way around to it when Mrs. Wheatley gave a piercing shriek.

"Run, Netta, there's a bear!"

A bear! Netta was not prepared to tangle with a bear. She gave one agonized thought to her pail of berries that were just out of reach, then turned and fled into the pasture. Mrs. Wheatley joined her and they fairly flew back to their wagon.

"Oh Netta, I've left my pail there. Wasn't that foolish? But I can't go back to get it. Look! The bear is still there."

Netta looked to where Mrs. Wheatley was pointing with a trembling finger and, sure enough, she caught a glimpse of brown fur through the bushes. She could hear the snapping and crunching of twigs as the huge animal moved about. The two women caught their placidly grazing horse and hitched up as fast as they could when their hands were shaking so badly. They drove back up the cart track to the farmyard.

As Mr. Henderson was no longer near the house, they did not stop to say goodbye. They drove home very sorry not to have any berries for their dinner that night, but they consoled themselves that at least they had a good story to dine out on. Indeed, when Netta later married and had children, she would tell them her bear story to impress upon them how wild Edmonton had been in the days when she was growing up.

That might have been the end of my story but it isn't.

One August day a good many years later, when Netta's daughter, Vonda, was seventeen years old, Mr. Henderson came into town on a honey-selling trip. He dropped in at the Wilson house—Netta was Mrs. Wilson now—and sat down in the kitchen for a visit. Her kitchen was a big, square, sunny room, the usual place for informal visits. Old Mr. Henderson settled down over his cake and coffee and mentioned that the raspberry crop was particularly good this year. "Best it's been in years! I remember just one other summer like this for raspberries. That was before you were born, missy," he said to Vonda. "We ate so many raspberries that summer I thought we'd turn pink, and we canned fifty quarts of them! I had a good thing going that summer. Lots of people dropped by to pick raspberries that August. I had this old bearskin with the head and claws still on it and I used to drape that over my shoulders and crawl about in the raspberry bushes. Lots of people ran out of there screaming about bears. It sure saved me a lot of time picking berries!"

I heard this story when my mother and I went to tea with Mrs. Vonda Wilson Smith. Vonda Smith was ninety then and has since died. She said Netta had married in 1904 and the story happened before that, when Netta was 16 or 17, hence my guess at the year 1900. Vonda Smith gave me permission to tell this story and I pass on that permission with the provision that tellers acknowledge that they got it from Mrs. Smith via me.

MAMA AND THE BEAR

Kathy Jessup

My mother is terrified of bears. Everyone should be somewhat afraid of bears. They are wild animals after all, and if they feel threatened they can certainly hurt you, so it is best to stay out of their way. But with my mother, it goes beyond fear and reaches almost phobic proportions.

When I was little, I lived in a small village up in the northern bush country and we saw bears quite often. If you went hiking or fishing, you'd regularly come across black bears. They were often found scavenging at campsites along the highway, especially when humans weren't wise about garbage disposal. In fact one summer, my home town had over forty bears dining at the garbage dump. It was a tourist attraction! Most people were used to dealing with them. My mom was not.

I remember one summer vacation at our cabin there was a bear lingering about all the places up and down the lakeshore. We were at the cabin alone with mom as our dad had to work. Now picture this poor woman who had six kids under her wing. She was out in a little cabin in the northern woods with a bear prowling around her backyard. It was scary.

My dad had anticipated that a situation like this might occur. Many northerners keep guns at the ready for just this type of ordeal. My mother wasn't about to wield a gun, as she didn't know the first thing about firearms. My dad said, "You don't need a gun anyway. What you want is a dog. All you need is a yappy dog that will bark like crazy whenever a bear comes around. It'll scare off the bear and you'll have no problems."

And so Buddy the family dog became our protector.

My mom was not convinced that one medium-sized mutt was enough protection against a several-hundred-pound, wild, hungry black bear. What if the bear hurt the dog? Our family would be devastated. Although she didn't want to use a real gun, she wondered whether a cap gun might be a little added insurance. *If bears are scared away by a noise, then maybe loud bangs from a cap gun might be just the right thing!*

The next grocery day, my mother went to town and bought herself a cap gun.

I should mention now that my two teenaged brothers were, in fact, gun crazy. They had experience with smaller gauge shotguns— shooting tin cans off fence posts and rousing up grouse. They were more than happy to volunteer to be our protectors. My mom would have none of it. She knew a small shotgun would not kill a bear, and she didn't want a wounded, angry bear prowling around her property. No. The more she thought about it, the more she was sure the cap gun was her best defense.

She brought the cap gun home, loaded it, and placed it (along with some extra rounds of caps) on the top of the fridge, next to the door. She forbade any of us to go near it. And then . . . we waited for the next bear sighting.

Now the thing about gun crazy boys is . . . you can't have something fun like a cap gun in the house and not expect them to use it. Whenever mom was away from the cabin on a walk, or berry-picking, the boys would head straight for the cap gun and fire off a few rounds. It was great fun until mom decided to test the gun a few days later. She brought it down and held it out to fire. Click. Click. It was empty. She was not happy. She reloaded the gun, lectured us to leave it alone, and placed it back on top of the fridge. Again we waited for the bear.

Sure enough, the day came.

There was the unmistakable sound of garbage cans banging around out back. We were all in the cabin at the time, including the dog. Buddy immediately began barking and running around as if to say, "Let me at him, let me at him!" My mother was safe with us inside the cabin but, for some reason, was compelled to confront the bear.

She opened the cabin door, and with the cap gun extended, she ventured onto the front step. She turned to face the bear. Mom hollered at us to stay inside so we watched the saga unfold from the cabin doorway.

The bear suddenly saw us and began to back away from the garbage cans. Mom fired off her first round of caps. Bang! Bang! Bang!

When the bear heard this he stopped. He looked curiously at the gun, and began lumbering toward our mom. We shrieked. The dog barked like crazy. The bear retreated.

Just to be sure, mom fired off another round of caps. Bang! Bang! Bang! The bear halted. Again he looked curiously at the gun and lumbered towards us. Again we shrieked. Again the dog barked. Again the bear retreated.

It was the darndest thing! This sequence repeated itself: my mother compelled to fire off her gun, the curious bear lumbering toward us, our shrieks, Buddy's yelps and barks, and the bear's retreat. Finally, my mother had fired all the caps. At this point Buddy managed to wriggle between our tangle of legs and out the door. Buddy, the little mutt, ran barking and snarling straight for the bear. He was ferocious! The bear took one look at the dog, turned tail, and ran pell-mell up the driveway, never to be seen again.

Come to think of it, we never saw that cap gun again either.

BELLY BUTTON FUZZ

Pearl-Ann Gooding

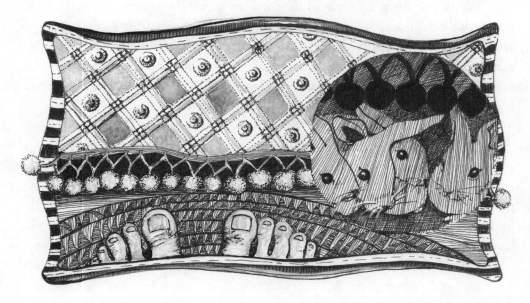

Cold Lake, today, is a booming town with a beautiful tourist area and park as well as a military base and a NATO training area. When my family was stationed at C.F.B. Cold Lake in 1958, the P.M.Q. (Private Married Quarters) that were issued to us had just had the foundation poured. The roads to Cold Lake were gravel; some people still tied their horses out front of the general store; it cost fifteen cents to see a movie. The area was considered semi-isolated only because people from elsewhere didn't bother to come up and see that it was totally isolated. Our whole life took place on the military base: our home, entertainment, education, and work. Simple, silly things were highlights of fun in our home. They form my fondest memories. Let me share one of these memories with you.

My dad worked a lot and seemed to be involved in a world that was more serious and important than that of family life and kids. We kids knew that we had our sphere and he had his. Occasionally, though, Dad would get the sillies and search us out for fun.

Part of the military uniform my dad wore was a cotton undershirt. After a full day of wear, it tended to pill and little balls of cotton congregated in his belly button. Sometimes, after a long day at work, he walked in through the back porch door and, if one of us kids was in the kitchen, he would make eye contact, hold you in his vision, and break out in a devilish grin. Like a little boy revealing a secret treasure to a captive audience, he reached down and took hold of the bottom of his undershirt with both hands. He slowly lifted his shirt, gathering the material in his fingers—eye contact totally secured and an impish expression on his face.

We stood transfixed, excited, terrified; unable to move or make a sound. We were predator and prey, knowing what was coming, unable to stop it. When his protruding belly was exposed, he opened and closed his forefinger and thumb like a crab's pincher claw. He started high above his shoulder and slowly moved his pinching fingers toward his belly button. When the claw finally reached his belly button, he triumphantly pinched out the cotton fuzz and gave a deep menacing howl of glee!

The sound broke the petrifying spell that had been cast on us, and we screamed and ran in circles all over the house. We screeched and he howled a deep, laughing "mooouuahhh ahhh ahhh!" Dad lifted his leg slowly and gently swung it forward to land on a partially crouched leg. It was like watching a slow-motion, creeping gorilla. He would lift, swing, slide his leg, and we would run, bump, and scream. In the midst of this chaos, we kids tore upstairs to my sister's bedroom, slammed the door, and darted beneath her double bed. We scrambled to find the furthest spot away from the edge of the bed. We were sure Dad would never find us as we pushed, pulled, shoved, and squished one another. Then Dad ascended the stairs, each step creaking, and now in a scary drawn out voice: "Here . . . I . . . come . . . mooouuahh ahh ahh!" We screamed louder and fought harder for the furthest spot. We heard him stop just outside the bedroom door, making his last step or two dramatically loud. He grabbed the door knob and turned. We plastered the side of our heads to the floor so we could see. The door swung open and knocked against the wall a few times until it hung still. We saw his feet. Fear, silence, no breath, eyes so big they threatened to pop out of their sockets. With the same creeping, gorilla gait he took one step into the room. And then, another. Screams stuck in our throats. Our mouths opened but no sound came out. In-breath—no exhale. Another step forward, another, then—stop. His pant cuffs crinkled on the top of his feet as he lowered himself to the floor. We saw his hands hit the floor, then one knee, then the other. We held our breath as he lowered his head to the floor. Only when our eyes connected with his, did we know we were found. We squealed and flung our bodies to squish ourselves to the furthest spot again.

There were four of us under there—eight legs and eight arms kicking and swinging. He latched onto one limb and pulled. We screamed and kicked as if our lives were about to end. Then, suddenly, the siblings who seconds before pushed and pulled to compete for a safe spot, now grabbed and held firmly to the one who was caught. But we were no match for Dad's strength. Slowly and surely a body followed the limb as Dad dragged it out. Slowly and surely the reality that our sibling was caught sank into our awareness and we relented. Once the victim was out from under the bed, Dad would scatter the belly button fuzz over the body, especially the facial area, as if performing an ancient ritual. At this point the rest of us knew it was a done deal. We crawled out and scampered away, leaving the victim to endure the ritual deed like a rabbit in the clutches of a lion. *Oh well, you are already dead and being eaten—no sense in trying to rescue you now.*

In between our silly sessions of apish glee we often asked Dad what he did with the belly button fuzz that he accumulated. He told us that he had a pillowcase in his closet. He put the fuzz in it every day and when it was full Mom would sew it up. "What do you think pillows are made of?" he asked.

SEEDS IN A
POCKET

OF SOAP AND WATER

Antonietta Cimello-Dennis

When I tell people that doing laundry is one of my favourite chores, they think that I am joking but I'm not.

I love the scent and feel of newly laundered items as I fold and smooth them. I feel satisfied when I see stacks of clean towels and linens and neatly folded piles of my family's clothing.

Often, when I am doing laundry in the comfort of my home—waiting for one load to finish the spin and another to finish tumbling in the dryer, my mind is flooded with memories of laundry days with my mother over fifty years ago.

We lived in Calabria, a region in southern Italy, up until the late 1950s. We washed our laundry at one of our village's nearby rivers, using slabs of not-so-gentle homemade soap and a rock for a washboard.

The women took along the younger children and packed a picnic lunch. We had fun while our mothers worked. We played, splashed in the shallow water, collected frogs and bugs, and picked wild strawberries and flowers. It was a day of no chores for us.

Best of all was lunch. At noon the women spread white tablecloths on the grass and laid out the food. We all ate together. What a feast! There was cheese and sausages, olives, roasted sweet peppers, salad with anchovies, tomatoes, fruit, nuts, and a variety of breads.

After lunch the women gossiped and told stories. This was a chance for the young single girls to go behind the enormous rocks to bathe and wash their hair. With the help of a slab of the not-so-gentle homemade soap, their feet and hands were free of stains from harvesting grapes and olives, at least until the next day. Having clean shiny hair would surely guarantee whistles of admiration from the boys standing in the piazza at the coffee bar.

I remember one day in particular. I was five or six years old. It was a beautiful autumn day. We had just finished our lunch when one of the women remarked how white and spotless her laundry was, as if the water had some magic power. My mother replied, "Oh, but it is true! In fact there is a story about the water and the magic of this river."

The women said eagerly, "Please tell it to us, Maria."

And so my mother began:

"Many years ago in our village there lived a beautiful girl. She was an orphan. Her name was Viola. She worked for the signori and every year at the time of the grape harvest she would work long hours, picking grapes and crushing them with her feet, as was the custom. Poor Viola! By the end of the season her hands and feet were a deep blue purple, just like her name.

"Now one day the Count of Monterosso came to our village to look for workers, and, would you believe it, he saw Viola with her shining black hair and eyes like laughing stars. The poor man was smitten. He took her hand and said, ' Please come with me to my castle and be my wife.'

"Viola ran home to pack her things and bid goodbye to her family. She was ready to go with the count faster than you can say 'grape juice'.

"Upon arriving at the castle, the count asked his servants to prepare a bath for Viola and to bring her the most beautiful garments to wear. She washed in water scented with spikenard (lavender) and soap made with milk and honey. However, she could not wash the grape stains from her hands and feet, no matter how hard she scrubbed.

"She clothed herself in the lovely garments and, with tears in her eyes, she stood before the count. He was thrilled with her beauty until he saw her hands and feet, and then his face fell. This caused Viola to cry all the more. How could she wear the beautiful, white wedding gown and golden slippers when her hands and feet were stained?

"The count summoned the wise men of his council, but no one knew how to solve the problem since Viola had bathed and scrubbed to no avail. They all knew that the count would be the object of much ridicule if his bride came to the altar with the deep dye of grapes on her hands and feet. They agreed that the wedding could not possibly take place.

"But then, just when Viola was giving up all hope, she remembered her secret place behind the enormous rock by the river—the place where she had once washed her stained hands and feet after the harvest. She told this to the count. He immediately called a servant to make ready for the journey to the rock. They travelled through the village and the olive grove that led to the steep narrow road and down to the river. There, Viola slipped quickly behind the big rock and washed with a slab of not-so-gentle homemade soap. The stains on her hands and feet disappeared just like the stains on the white linens.

"How pleased the count was! The next day there was much rejoicing at the castle, for the count and Viola were united in marriage.

"Did they live happily ever after? Yes, they did!"

The story was over and the laundry had dried. The women helped each other fold it neatly, placing it in baskets. As they carried the baskets on their heads, they walked up the narrow winding path through the olive grove leading to the village and their homes.

I wonder . . . was there magic in the water to make our laundry spotless and bright? Was there magic in the water to take the grape and olive stains from hands and feet? Or . . . was it the slabs of not-so-gentle homemade soap . . . ?

I came to Edmonton from Italy with my parents and two younger brothers when I was seventeen. Three of my mother's seven brothers were already in Canada. My mother decided that we should emigrate, as one of her brothers had agreed to sponsor our family. My father was not in favour of this. He was an avid reader and knew some geographical facts about Canada, especially that Alberta had long and frigid winters. But mother was convinced that if her brothers could afford to include a dollar whenever they wrote a letter to us, she should emigrate so that her children could have a better future too.

CAPE BRETON WAKE

Rose Steele

Most people who are raised on Cape Breton Island get homesick as soon as they cross over the Canso Causeway that joins Cape Breton to the mainland. Not me! Right after graduating from university, I spread my wings and headed for Alberta. I enjoyed the adventure of the mountains, the Stampede, teaching in Calgary classrooms, and making new friends. However, after living in Alberta for thirty-five years, I still have the Caper accent. I hear a name and I think: *that is a home name.* A Cape Breton story, tune, or song whisks me right back to the island. I love that I have an Alberta address, but home is where my roots are: the stories, told in a particular rhythm and cadence, the ability to laugh when others would cry, and a simple, grounded philosophy of life, remind me of my Cape Breton roots. Though I am an Albertan, I view the world through a Caper's eyes.

If you've visited Cape Breton Island, you know the people there have a unique way of speaking, acting, and viewing the world. There is a definite code of behaviour. If someone strays from *The Code,* the typical comment by witnesses is, "I wouldn't call him a Caper, would you?"

The everyday lives of Capers are rich in folklore, superstitions, and stories of the supernatural, passed on through Celtic and French ancestors. When I was a child, I heard the elders speak about encounters with ghosts, haunted houses, and forerunners of death. These stories were spoken in truthful and sincere tones. Superstitions and Christian beliefs were intertwined to become a unique Cape Breton experience.

When someone in the community died, the wake was conducted according to this unique tradition. The wake was usually held at the residence of the deceased. A spray of flowers hung on the front door indicating the occurrence of the wake. Custom dictated that the sun must set three times on the body before burial. It was required that someone be in the room with the body at all times in order to protect it from evil spirits. Touching the body was believed to be a way of erasing any negative memories of the wake.

When I was seven years old, my aunt by marriage passed away. Therefore, out of respect for the deceased, I was excused from school so that I could attend the wake which was held at our house. I was happy to be let out of school and it was exciting to have our house full of people.

I vividly remember this particular wake. There is a scene in my mind that will be crystal-clear forever. The grey casket arrives. It is placed on a stand in our living room under the piano windows. The kneeler is placed in front of the casket. As the casket is opened, I see Jessie dressed in her white lace wedding gown with her blue rosary beads wound around her waxy hands. The large spray of flowers on the casket and the wreaths and bouquets fill the room with their gagging sweet scents. I hear the people who are sitting or standing in clusters talking in hushed tones. I sense the air of anxiety that hangs in the room. The relatives are concerned about how Jessie's sister, Rita, will handle her loss.

There is a squeezed silence after someone announces that Rita and her dad are coming. I scurry to the front sun porch. As they round the corner of the house I see Mr. Power with his arm protectively around his daughter's shoulder, physically supporting her as they proceed to the back door. Rita's face is very pale and her whole body is trembling. As they enter the back door and continue on to the living room, I position myself to observe the event.

As soon as Rita enters the living room, she breaks from her dad and throws herself on the casket. She lunges her two hands onto Jessie's shoulders and lifts and shakes her as she screams, "Jessie get up, get up, you're not dead!"

Instantly, I bolt. I run out of the room, up the stairs, down the hall, open the door to the attic, and climb the ladder. I crunch myself into a small ball. Even though I cover my ears I can still hear her anguished screams.

When all is quiet, I am drawn back to the living room where I see my aunt, Sister Mary Henry, soothing Rita. She cradles Rita as she softly and gently reminds her that Jessie would not like this display of behaviour. Then the doctor arrives and gives Rita a long needle in the arm. Like magic, she relaxes; her dad leads her out of the room and takes her home.

The scary part of the wake is over. Now it's time for friends and relatives to liven things up. Since the wake is held for three days and people sit around the clock, the community informally arranges to have refreshments available for the mourners. Most people bring something along for the lunch—sandwiches, brownies with mocha icing, banana, lemon, or cinnamon loaves and pork pies which have a shortbread shell filled with dates, topped with maple icing, and capped with a walnut. The kettle never rests as strong black tea is constantly brewing.

During the day, while some mourners take shifts staying with the body, the others gather in the kitchen speaking in hushed voices about the circumstances concerning the death. They reminisce about the deceased, exchange family stories, and sip tea. Someone sings a mournful song.

In the wee hours of the morning, there is a subtle change. While some mourners still take shifts with the body, the others gather in the kitchen. Tea brews on the stove but many exchange teacups for glass tumblers which contain something even stronger than Cape Breton brewed tea. Their tongues are loosened: humour, gossip, and nonsense spice the conversation. The wake becomes a party where people who haven't seen each other since the last wake enjoy each other's company. Friends offer grieving loved ones nourishment and comfort for body and soul. The healing begins.

RAMBLES FROM MY LIFE UP NORTH

Catherine MacKenzie

Although many of Alberta's cities and towns have grown significantly in the past three decades, few can compare to the explosion witnessed in Fort McMurray due to the development of the area's oil sands.

When Don and I first arrived in this northern frontier in 1974, there were no traffic lights, the streets were gravel, and people met at the post office to pick up mail. It was a young town with historic roots. Its population was young and predominantly male. Although it was home to some, many came to make a buck and move on. There was a movie theatre and a few restaurants, but we mostly entertained in our homes. We enjoyed taking extension courses at Keyano College which was housed in trailer units. I remember huddling in my down parka as the snow fell and I watched a barbeque demonstration in the early dark by the light of the street lamp. Some friendships were forged that would last a lifetime, but people came and went and some relationships never had the opportunity to mature. Still, there was a feeling of community. We recognized many of the people at the blueberry festival and invariably met someone we knew whenever we ventured outside. Cold as it was, we weren't deterred from outside activities. We were, in a sense, bound together by our ability to survive in this harsh climate.

Work again drew us to the community in 1986. The road from Edmonton was paved. There was the familiar smell of oil in the air and the view as we drove down Beacon Hill was as spectacular as ever, but the town had mushroomed. Streets and houses were being built at a frantic pace to try and keep up with the demand for housing. New subdivisions sprang up across the river. We were thrilled to discover that the theatre at Keyano College was a first-class venture that attracted productions from around the world. The college facilities were permanent and beautiful. A distinctive purple residence housed students who wanted to live on campus. A combined high school–YMCA facility offered additional indoor recreation opportunities. A new library offered programs for patrons of all ages. People came and went, but now some stayed.

I recognized a few faces when we returned yet again in 2003. The demand for housing was greater than ever and prices rivaled the highest in the nation. Men working shifts shared beds in basement suites. Construction was evident everywhere you turned. A large transient population still filled the camps; traffic leaving the city on Friday evening and returning on Sunday was a nightmare. Recreation facilities were at a premium and building new ones was a priority for mayoralty candidates.

Fort McMurray is still a new and raw place, ever growing, ever changing. It's an exciting place to live. Recreational and cultural opportunities abound. People are retiring here, but many still come only until the job is finished and then move on. I will be one of them, but I will always carry a bit of this northern community with me as I remember the beauty of the northern lights and the warmth of the friends I made here. Let me share a few notes from my life up here in northern Alberta.

Alberta Metaphor

I grew up in a part of New York where it's hard to tell where one town ends and another begins. What a shock when I moved to Alberta with all this space. As I approached Grande Prairie for the first time, I saw a small sign, a white wooden arrow with the word *Alaska* inscribed in black. To reach Alaska I needed merely to turn right at Grande Prairie!

It wasn't until our move to Fort McMurray that I really came to appreciate Alberta's wide-open space. There were not many signs of civilization on the five-hour drive between Fort McMurray and Edmonton. We had a choice of stopping for gas and a bite to eat at Wandering River or Grassland. Long as it was, the trip was beautiful. If blowing snow didn't blind us, we often saw fantastic displays of northern lights or beautiful rainbows . . . sometimes with double bows. There were always coyotes and birds of prey.

Don and I rented a place on the top floor of an apartment in Fort McMurray. No longer would we be disturbed by the sounds of people above us. Imagine my surprise when daily I heard noisy thumping overhead. At first I thought it was the caretakers doing some sort of repair work, but days passed, snow came, and the thumping continued. I decided to investigate.

Enormous black birds with wingspans of more than a metre clattered on the roof. They looked somewhat like the crows back home, but they were big, really big. In fact, I learned that the raven is the largest songbird in the world. Yes, a songbird, though I'd hardly classify their raucous guttural croak as a song!

The raven is also the largest completely black bird. Its jet-black feathers remind me of long winter nights in the north when there is so little light that it's hard to feel motivated. But even in the invigorating, long days of summer I struggled to rouse myself from bed to make breakfast and pack a lunch so that Don could catch the five-fifteen bus. I wasn't very happy when he reported that someone was swiping his lunch. He'd put it out on the porch to keep cool and come lunchtime the entire bag would be missing . . . not a crumb of evidence. Surreptitiously he checked what the other men were eating but could catch no one. Annoyed that his lunch continued to be pilfered, Don set up a stakeout.

The thief was of course, our friend raven. Carrion eaters by choice, ravens will eat just about anything, including pinecones, spiders, fruit, garbage, and egg salad sandwiches apparently. I understand how they got a reputation for being greedy, mischievous tricksters. I forgive them their mischievous nature as I marvel at the sight of their coal-black wings painted on an expanse of big blue sky. I thrill at their aerial acrobatics and their raucous song. I have lived in Canada for more than thirty years and I am still awed by this beautiful bird. The sense of freedom and space that ravens evoke as they soar through the open sky has come to represent Alberta to me.

Voices

Back in 1975 you didn't need a demographic study to know that most women in Fort McMurray were of childbearing age and that a good portion of them were pregnant. I was one of them and, except for the morning sickness, I loved every moment of being pregnant. I loved seeing the shape of a tiny foot pushing out against my belly. I loved the cradle that Don was making and was confident that the pegboard and tools would be gone by the time we brought our baby home. And I loved the names that we had picked out for our first child.

I was going to be one of those women who merely call their children's names to have them come running. They never have to raise their voices. I was going to be that kind of mother. I would respond to my child's voice and she to mine.

The reality was that not only could I not differentiate my daughter's voice— I could not recognize her amongst others in the nursery.

You must realize that where there are lots of pregnant women there are lots of newborns. Although Fort McMurray was, and still is, a multi-ethnic community, most of the babies had straight, black hair that stuck straight up—or that's how it seemed to me. Luckily, the General Hospital saw fit to wrap the infants in pink or blue blankets depending on gender, so I had only to pick mine from half the baby population.

I was admiring my beautiful baby, less than two days old, through the glass of the nursery, when I saw that she had a large red mark on the side of her face. I cried out in alarm. The woman next to me assured me that it was just a birthmark and would fade over time. I was not to be calmed so easily. "But it wasn't there yesterday," I protested. The woman assured me that it most certainly had been. After a few more remonstrations on my part, it became apparent that the baby in question was hers. My daughter, Amber, was the black-haired girl in the pink blanket in the next bassinet. Her beautiful blue eyes were a distinguishing feature, so when she woke up I knew my baby.

Well, I can tell you, I was not about to make the same mistake with my second child. I went to the hospital prepared. Amber and a friend made several colourful stuffed toys for the new baby and I intended to put them at the end of the bassinet. I'd be able to recognize this baby awake or asleep! But, you know, God knew my heart. He knew my weaknesses and my need. I did dress up the bassinet with toys, but our second daughter, Julie, was born with striking red hair. There was no mistaking her.

I am gifted with three wonderful children who all stand out in a crowd—not so much because of their appearance, but because of their personalities. I may not have been that mother that I dreamed of being—the one who called and her children came running. But when I observe my grown-up children, I notice that I can hear my voice in them and theirs in me.

DOCTOR KNOW-IT-ALL

Heidi Price

A ship docked in Halifax Harbour on May 6, 1951. Its occupants, several hundred European immigrants, had been at sea for nine days. They came from places such as Germany, Sweden, Holland, Norway, and Czechoslovakia. A few remained in Halifax, but the majority boarded the Canadian Pacific Railway train in order to reach destinations elsewhere in Canada. One family, from Germany— a mother, father, and their two young girls—was destined for Western Canada. Like all the others, though they carried few belongings, they brought a treasure of memories, traditions, and stories from their homeland. The train ride was long and, as time passed, confinement on the train took its toll. The father resorted to telling stories—old, familiar stories so well known by the children of Germany. I was the older of these two young girls and my father asked me for my request of a story. My choice was "Doktor Allwissend" or "Doctor Know-It-All."

Once upon a time there was a poor farmer by the name of Krebs—in English that's Crab. To earn extra money Herr Crab loaded his wagon with wood to sell, then mounted his cart and guided his two oxen to town. One day he stopped at the town doctor's home and unloaded the wood. The doctor's wife, Frau Doktor, paid him the money in the doorway of their home. Herr Crab noticed the doctor wining and dining at the table. A most delicious aroma filled the room. Herr Crab wished that he, too, had become a doctor. The doctor noticed the farmer peering at him from the entryway. *"Kommen Sie herein!"* he said and beckoned with his hand.

Herr Crab stepped carefully into the hallway. "Oh, how I, also, would like to become a doctor," he sighed.

The doctor smiled and replied, "*O ja,* that will happen soon."

"Please, tell me what I need to do," Herr Crab pleaded.

"First, buy yourself an ABC book—you know the kind—with a picture of a rooster in the first few pages.

"Second, sell your wagon and your two oxen and with that money buy yourself some clothes and whatever else a doctor needs.

"Thirdly, dear Crab, make a sign with the words, *I am Doctor Know-It-All,* and have it nailed above your door."

Herr Crab did as he was advised. He bought himself an ABC book, the kind with a picture of a rooster on it. He sold his oxen and wagon and bought the things a doctor needs, and he hung out a sign that said: *I am Doctor Know-It-All.* He did a bit here and there—whatever a doctor usually does—and was feeling quite proud of himself. Then, one day, a wealthy man encountered a misfortune. A large amount of money was stolen from him.

Doctor Know-It-All was informed and soon the unfortunate gentleman who had been robbed of his money came to pay the doctor a visit.

"*Doktor Allwissend?*"

"*Ja,* I am the one."

The two men discussed the situation and it was arranged that Doctor Know-It-All would accompany the gentleman to his home in order to locate the money. "Oh *ja,* but Grete, my wife, must come along," announced Doctor Know-It-All.

The gentleman agreed and shortly after, Doctor Know-It-All and his wife Grete travelled with the gentleman to his home. A beautiful table was set for the three of them to dine. The gentleman invited them to sit down and enjoy a fine meal before embarking on solving the money mystery. Gladly, Grete and her husband sat down. Soon the first waiter came into the room with a big bowl of delicious food. The doctor nudged his wife and pointed, "Grete, that was the first one," (the first of several anticipated waiters). The waiter, however, understood the comment to mean that he was the first thief, which, in fact, he was. The waiter was afraid and when he returned to the kitchen he said to his comrades, "The doctor knows everything. He said I am the first one."

The second waiter did not want to enter the dining room but he had little choice. As he brought the next bowl of food the doctor again nudged his wife and pointed. "Grete, that is the second one."

The waiter quickly set the bowl on the table and fled to the kitchen. The third waiter appeared in the dining room and he did not fare any better.

"Grete, that is the third one." The third waiter fled the room.

The fourth waiter had to carry the biggest bowl. The bowl was covered with a lid. Now the gentleman, who had observed his guests with a smile, asked the doctor to guess what might be in the bowl. (It was actually a very large cooked crab.) Doctor Know-It-All looked at the bowl and became exceedingly concerned. After a considerable pause he put his hands on his face and exclaimed, "Oh me, poor old Crab!"

When the gentleman heard this, he shouted with excitement, "He knows it . . . he knows what is in the bowl. He will also know who stole my money!"

Meanwhile the fourth waiter became extremely afraid and begged the doctor to come into the kitchen—on the pretense he wanted to show him other such large crabs. Once in the kitchen, the four confessed that they had committed the crime. They were more than willing to return the money and even give a large sum on top of it, if only Doctor Know-It-All would not tell the gentleman that they were the thieves. They led the doctor to the kitchen cupboard where they had hidden the money. Doctor Know-It-All was now quite satisfied and went out to speak with the gentleman.

"Sir, now I will look in my book to see where the stolen money could be."

Meanwhile, the fifth waiter, unknown to the others, crawled into the large, cold brick oven in order to eavesdrop on what else this wise doctor might know. The doctor stood in front of the gentleman, opened his ABC book and flipped through the pages to find the one with the rooster.

"Oh *ja*, I know you are in there somewhere and you must come out!" the doctor spoke as he thumbed the book.

The fifth waiter, who was hiding in the oven, heard the doctor searching for the rooster, and thought the doctor meant for *him* to come out. Full of fear he jumped out of the oven and exclaimed, "The man knows everything!"

Doctor Know-It-All retrieved the stolen money for the gentleman but did not tell him who had stolen it. He received a substantial reward not only from the gentleman but from the thieves as well. Dr. Know-It-All became a wealthy and famous man. I wonder if he wined and dined in a room filled with delicious aromas while some poor fellow unloaded wood from a cart.

This story is liberal adapted from a favourite childhood book of mine entitled Deutsche Maerchen, *a collection of tales published in 1939 by Cigaretten-Bilderdienst in Hamburg, Germany, and gathered by Dr. Paul Alverdes of Munich. It's a traditional German tale first collected by the Grimm Brothers.*

THE GOOD RED EARTH

Lisa Hurst-Archer

This story was trolled from the waters of my childhood memories. Is it my
story, my mother's, grandmother's, or grandfather's story? I give it to you
with the hope that you will cast your net and draw in a story of your own.

Over the river and through the woods to grandmother's house we go, the horse knows
the way . . . actually we're in the car. We're packed in tight. My brother is a pest.
It's a long stretch on the 401 through Ontario. There's no air conditioning.

Over the river and through the woods and all the way up through Quebec, to the
ferry line in Tormentine, we'll get to the Island yet.

We're crossing the deep blue Northumberland Strait, sun on our hair, salt
wind in our faces. We lean our necks and stare to capture the moment it comes
into view . . . and then . . . it rises up out of the waters before us: the red earth and
leafy green of Prince Edward Island.

The last leg of the journey is excruciatingly long. Finally, we turn on to a dirt
road and there on a hill in the distance is a cedar shake house with gingerbread

trim. The wood is weathered grey, every last fleck of whitewash blown free, borne away on the winds of an Atlantic gale. The house is old. My grandparents are old.

There's a long line of chestnut trees waving their leafy hands at us. The car pulls up the rutted lane to a stop. We spill out and my grandmother is coming through the wooden screen door. She's wiping her hands on her calico apron. She's twinkling her eyes at me.

Come on in. Come on in . . .

The kitchen's the largest room in the house. There's a big wood stove and a table with a checkered oilcloth. There are a couple of day beds along the back wall and china birds collected from tea boxes perched on the window sill. The most familiar thing about this room is the silent symphony of scent—wild berries, yellow wax beans, thick black tea, milk in a tin—all is infused with the scent of wood smoke and wrapped in the sweet, earthy tang of red soil.

We make a lot of ruckus hauling our luggage up the big wood staircase, fighting over who gets which feather bed, screeching and holding our noses at the sight of chamber pots. The walls in the upstairs rooms are warm—years of summer heat soaked into plaster, the plaster sifted away, leaving only layer upon layer of yellowed wall paper and paste. When we've claimed our sleeping territories and unpacked our bags, we head outdoors to swing on a rope in the barn *sunlight shadow sunlight shadow*. We chase wild kittens. We work the pump to fill a bucket with clear cold water and haul it in to our grandmother.

After supper and the dishes, the relatives come to set for a while. There's strong tea and thick bread to daub into molasses in saucers. My grandfather is playing the mouth organ and someone is splacking on the spoons. My grandmother is tapping her toes. I can see she got those lines at the corners of her eyes from smiling. The room fills with soft, sweet singing. When the music dies down these folk do not shy away from a room of people and no sound.

Soundlessly soundlessly russet skinned white fleshy gems are formed in the good red earth while we sit in my grandmother's kitchen.

Potatoes are the lifeblood of these people. When the talk is taken up again, it's of rain or lack, frost too soon or too late—and did you know the big agri-businesses are buying up Island farms and they don't even rotate the crop to let a field lie fallow now and then, and did you know they're selling potatoes down in

Charlottetown in clear plastic bags and piling them up under the bright lights, and whoever heard of exposing potatoes to the light on purpose?

I knew that my grandfather stored his potatoes in the dark. Down in the cellar. When I played around the farmyard, I was aware of the mound of earth with the sloping wood cellar door. One time my mother opened the door so that I could climb down the shaft of daylight on the stairs which were slabs of red sandstone hauled up from the coast. At the bottom step, I was startled by the thick, soft, moist dark. I heard the earth's dark breath. I heard whispered stories in the clay walls. Joy—an abundant harvest. Disappointment—the market price of potatoes sinking. Hope—if we hold them back and store them a little longer, prices will rise. Desperation—there's not a better price, there's not a better day.

My mother told me once how she and her nine sisters would follow in a line like geese pecking the ground behind their father to harvest potatoes by hand. They'd pile them up in the cart for the horse to haul and unload in the cellar— thousands and thousands of tumbling potatoes. The girls would clean the potatoes in sand by the light of a coal oil lantern. They would sort them into burlap sacks and sew up the sacks with a big needle making sure to leave two ears so their father could haul them back onto the cart and take them to the train yard to sell; my grandfather hopeful to be paid the value of a year's worth of bone wearying work.

One time, he went off with the harvest heaped high in the cart and left his family to await his return for days. My grandmother must have known he'd been into the drink. There were men who had stills out in the woods, brewing up hot liquor potions from potatoes. Once every couple of years, he'd up and disappear. My grandmother would sit in the chair by the stove and wait through the night. In the morning, she would be red-eyed, silent. My mother would have to skirt carefully around the woman who was her mother. She could feel the silent heat falling like waves from her mother's body. She might be flailed on the back of the head with a broom for being too dreamy-eyed or slow to carry water.

Two, three, four days her father would be gone. She could see lines of worry being drawn and etched on her mother's face. Where was he? The man who felled trees, loaded them on the cutter, hauled them home, and split them, enough to warm the big old house through a long cold winter; the man who farmed their land and got them through another season. Where had he gone off to with their potatoes? Potatoes that were seeded, hoed, harvested, cleaned, sorted, and bagged with the help of those he'd left behind.

That night my mother dreamed she heard him come home. In the morning, she crept down cellar and found him there. The strong, gentle, magnificent man that was her father looked to her like a broken toy tossed in a heap, a shameful, humble drunk. My mother shook him awake and he grinned.

"Daddy, where's the potato money?"

The money. His hands slapped at one pocket after another before triumphantly presenting a whack of paper bills. Peeling a good many from the top of the pile, he told her to hide some money away for a rainy day.

"You and me, we'll go to town, go into the shops. Buy something nice for your mama. Ice cream for you. French vanilla ice cream. Hide it away now. Hide it between the stones in the wall . . . and don't go telling anyone."

My mother grabbed the whole wad of money from her father and turned her back to him to climb the stairs. She ran round the house, through the kitchen door, and stood before the woman in the kitchen.

"Mama, Daddy's down cellar having a nap."

When my mother tells the story, I can feel the weight of her decision then. She, a young child, turned it all over like a stone. What could she do? She must roll that heavy stone to stop up a passageway to light—to a trip into town with her daddy, his strong hand in hers as they look in shop windows, ice cream melting in her mouth.

The little girl with the wide eyes and narrow shoulders must stand before her mother. She must thrust every dollar into her mother's hands and watch her mother's drawn face become soft again. The little girl knows she will never take that trip into town.

All of this was long ago. Now I hear my brother romping in the grass above. It occurs to me that he's likely to slam the door shut and leave me down here in the dark, so I climb the stone slab stairs and emerge into the world of sunlight. My brother is on an old tractor now, and he's the driver rolling over imaginary obstacles and cheering at every encounter. I fold the cellar door closed like it's the cover of a book and make sure it's locked before I walk around to the kitchen door. I imagine that I trace the path my mother trod with the money in her hands when she was a girl.

My grandfather is sitting at the kitchen table. He looks up from his reading and takes off his glasses, folds them, and places them on the checkered cloth. He shifts his chair to turn his whole body towards me. His eyes are clear and kind. He's wearing a blue wool cardigan with a white shirt underneath. He sits and waits without speaking to hear whatever I might say. The room is full and soft with silence. My grandmother comes through the screen door. She's twisted a corner of her apron to wipe the soil from the first new potatoes of summer.

Soundlessly soundlessly russet skinned white fleshy gems are forming in the good red earth even as I speak.

ABOUT THE AUTHORS

Jean Burgess was born in Calgary and spent her childhood years in the Peace Country of Alberta. She went to college in Olds and has lived throughout Alberta, the last thirty years in Edmonton. Jean says she draws on music and secrets of the natural world as key elements in her stories. She both creates her own stories and relies on the rich classic collections. Jean's tales circle the world: healing stories, history, horse stories, humour, folktales, native legends, and pioneer stories.

Antonietta Cimello-Dennis emigrated from Italy to Edmonton, Alberta, in 1959. According to church records, her family has resided in Capistrano, a small town in the Calabria region of southern Italy since the seventeenth century. Antonietta says her life in Canada revolves around her love for God, resulting in joyful relationships with family and friends. She thoroughly enjoys digging in the earth to create a beautiful and productive garden and loves to prepare food for anyone who comes through her door. She finds her involvement with the Parenting for the Future Association in Stony Plain, Alberta, fulfilling work. Antonietta tells stories to people of all ages.

Victor Daradick has been writing and telling his own stories for over thirty years. Many of his stories have appeared in books by Peter Gzowski, and he has told stories from Halifax to Vancouver. He lives in High Level, Alberta where the winters are long and the summers are beautiful.

Michael Ebsworth was raised in Alberta and currently lives in Lethbridge. He has roots in a culturally mixed ancestry and branches in the folk and story traditions of many parts of the world. He is at home with the telling of ancient ballads and myths and tall tales of the prairies. Michael has shared folk songs and stories for over forty years with people of all ages.

M. Jennie Frost lives in Edmonton, where both sets of her grandparents settled in 1906. Once a Latin teacher, Jennie ultimately decided in 1996 to devote herself to being a fulltime storyteller. She has told stories to adults and children at festivals, concerts, conferences, and schools in five provinces. Jennie is coordinator of Storytellers of Canada/Conteurs du Canada, and has published poetry and stories in anthologies and literary journals.

Pearl-Ann Gooding was born in Ottawa where her father was serving in the Canadian Air Force. When she was six weeks old, the family moved to C.F.B. Cold Lake, Alberta, where Pearl-Ann spent most of her childhood. Both her parents' families had been part of the exodus of members of The Church of Jesus Christ of Latter Day Saints that came to Alberta in the late 1800s to settle and build the famed temple in Cardston. One branch of her family has a long rich heritage in Canada going back many generations and blending with First Nation's people. Pearl-Ann is an avid quilter, potter, and willow weaver. She loves to create something out of nothing, turning a bare bones story into a rich and multi-layered tale. Pearl Ann lives happily with her family in Wainwright, Alberta, where she teaches and tells stories in schools and libraries.

Karen Gummo was born in Calgary's General Hospital like her father before her. Karen's Danish grandparents came to Canada in 1929. Her mother's family settled in the Markerville area of Alberta in 1889, after a gradual journey westward from Iceland beginning in 1875. Karen loves to tell about her great grandfather who walked to Airdrie from Markerville many times in the early years. When he needed to raise cash he went south to shear as many as one hundred sheep a day and walked home with a bag of flour and a bag of sugar on his back. He knew the best berry patches along the way and likely had a magpie or two to keep him company. Karen remains a passionate berry picker and lover of magpies. She tells stories to people of all ages.

Mary Hays was born and raised in Olds, Alberta, where she learned the art of storytelling around the kitchen table. Steaming coffee, she says, fueled her family's imagination when they told stories of growing up on the prairies in the 1930s. As a teacher, librarian, and storyteller, Mary is drawn to stories of her roots in the folk tales of Sweden and Scotland and the history of Alberta. She now teaches storytelling at the Southern Alberta Institute of Technology, directs community theatre, and adjudicates Speech Art Festivals.

Betty Hersberger was born in Saskatchewan and came to Alberta in 1975. She is passionate about words—in storytelling, in everyday speech, in the lyrics of songs, in every kind of writing, and in the etymology of words; their mutability and their constancy intrigue her. Betty's other loves include children, family, and the outdoors. She teaches literature and technical writing at the Southern Alberta Institute of Technology.

Lisa Hurst-Archer was born in Windsor, Ontario. Her mother's family came to Prince Edward Island from the British Isles and the island of Guernsey. Her father's people came to Waterloo County via Pennsylvania as part of a migration of Mennonites. Lisa loves to travel and share stories along the way but always likes to come home to the wide open skies of Alberta. She regards the Rocky Mountains and the rolling prairie as her good medicine. She lives in Calgary with her husband, five children, and a mutt dog. She facilitates workshops in communication, expression, and storytelling. Her mother would say, "She's been telling stories for a long time."

Kathy Jessup was born in Saskatchewan, was raised in northern British Columbia, and has spent all of her adult life in Alberta. After working for a decade as a broadcast journalist, Kathy began writing stories for children which in turn led her into the world of storytelling. She credits her love of storytelling to possessing the right gene pool, notably her Irish ancestry. She tours schools, libraries, and festivals across Canada telling original stories and leading workshops. Kathy lives in Edmonton with her husband, three daughters, and her very own bear dog.

Helen Lavender was born in Masefield, Saskatchewan, in 1934. Her mother had moved west from Ontario and her father from Nova Scotia. When Helen was two weeks old, her parents moved further west to the Alberta bush near Wildwood. They brought along her mother's fifteen-year-old brother, Helen's older brother, a cow and a calf, five horses, a crate of chickens and a dog. Helen grew up on Alberta farms and eventually received a teaching degree from the University of Alberta. She taught for a few years before raising her own large family. She loves horses, children, seniors, volunteering, writing, and storytelling. She tells stories in schools, libraries, and museums.

Catherine MacKenzie was born in Amherst, Massachusetts, where her father attended university. She grew up in New York where she met her Canadian husband while they were both attending university. She and Don moved to Grand Prairie, Alberta, in 1972. Since then, she's lived in many western Canadian towns and cities and was thrilled to become a citizen of Canada in 2004. Her days are filled with reading, storytelling, quilting, and puttering around on her flute. As a teacher-librarian by trade, she's passionate about children's stories—she fell in love with the art of oral storytelling by the bayous of Louisiana many years ago.

Marie Anne McLean was born in Winnipeg. Her father's ancestors came to Canada from Scotland in 1842. Her mother came to Canada as a Scottish war bride in 1945. Marie Anne was eight years old when oil was discovered on her great uncle's farm and her father moved his family west for work in the oil fields. Marie Anne is an elementary school teacher who loves the creative pursuits—painting, fabric arts, and storytelling. She loves to discover the stories of ordinary people. She tells original stories—about the prairie towns that are part of the background of so many of us—on radio, at festivals, schools, and concerts.

Heidi Price was born in Germany and has lived most of her life in Alberta. As a retired teacher, Heidi is filled with joy at the opportunities to be involved with children—playing with her grandchildren, tutoring, and telling stories to groups. She enjoys travelling with her husband—exploring Thai temples, journeying down the Nile, or hiking the Rocky Mountains with their beloved golden retriever.

Lana Skauge is a proud stubble jumper from Midale, Saskatchewan, who now resides in Calgary. Her love of the prairies and her commitment to finding the metaphor in this ever-changing landscape from her childhood has led this small town girl to a life of performing her original work across Canada and Great Britain. Her heritage is a mix of Norwegian and Appalachian farmers who she notes were not known for their complacency or spirit of compromise. Lana's straight-shooting ancestors have given her a strong sense of self that is celebrated and revitalized each time she creates. Lana is currently working on her eleventh commissioned work and has just finished touring one of her eighteen one-woman shows.

Louis Soop lives on the Blood reserve near Standoff. He's a painter, actor, Blackfoot language teacher, cultural consultant, dancer, and storyteller. He was also once a second lieutenant in the Armed Forces Reserves. While in Toronto in the 1960s, Louis married a "beautiful Irish girl from Newfoundland named Abby." In the 1970s Louis brought Abby back to the Blood Reserve, to a little piece of land that was his grandfather's. They built a house, raised horses and cows and kids. A few years ago, Louis and Abby became members of the Horn Society, one of the band's highest honours. Louis believes it is important to be an example to his people and help out any way he can. Over the years, he has developed a close relationship with elders, hearing and recording their stories to keep them for future generations.

Rose Steele is a Caper (from Cape Breton) who now calls Calgary home. She came to Calgary in 1966 to begin her teaching career. Time flew and a few years ago she traded full-time teaching for substituting. Now her joy is finding, collecting, and sharing children's literature with young people—down-home stories, stories that speak to the heart, or timeless folk tales that "make my being sing." She and her husband, Bob, have a beagle-basset, Maycee, who keeps them on their toes.

Heather Urness, illustrator, is a visual artist who has lived most of her life under a wide blue sky and is continually grateful for its inspiration.